Nebulous Seas

A Novella

Robert J. Bradshaw

Nebulous Seas

First Edition

Copyright © 2024 by Robert J. Bradshaw

All rights reserved.

Cover Art By Ronnie Jensen at: *Tegnemaskin.no*

ISBN: 978-1-7773763-8-3

Contents

Chapter 1

Come On In, the Water's Fine

Michigan, USA, 1996

The aging sedan jostled its way down the weathered road that ultimately led to the end of its lengthy journey. Everette Davis squinted as he saw the small green marker that indicated Lot Seventeen. Seeing the sign immediately made all the stress melt away. Finally, he could relax on his own terms.

No one for miles, he thought as he switched on the blinker and made a slow turn onto the unpaved road that served as a driveway. The vehicle followed the slight bend before the foliage gave way to a shabby lakeside cabin.

The water crashed against the rock-laden shore before pulling back and repeating the process. Everette blinked, for as far as the eye could see, water jutted out and touched the horizon. He felt a sense of awe upon taking in the scope of the great lake.

He parked his car just short of where the driveway met a

stone covered path and got out, taking a deep breath as he did so. The fresh October air circulated through his lungs and the scents of a crisp fall day lingered in his nostrils. He stretched before turning and grabbing his travel bag from the backseat.

Just the vacation I need, he thought as he locked his car and adjusted his grip on the bag.

Everette moved up the driveway and around the house, admiring the water as he did so. He studied the grey cloud cover lingering over the lake and knew it would rain. He ascended a short set of stairs that led to a shabby porch and heard the groan of the wood under his shoes.

He reached into his pocket and retrieved the cabin key, pulling open the screen door with his pinky finger. The sounds of the sea crept up behind him. The breeze ricocheted off the cabin's siding and sent a cool chill down his flannel jacket. He shivered as he put the key in the lock and turned the handle.

The hinges creaked as the door opened, revealing a small living area. He entered, his eyes scanning the room as he pushed the door closed behind him: A dusty red sofa, a dark fireplace with a brick chimney moving up into the ceiling along the left wall, and a kitchen area to the right.

Everette placed his bag on the couch and moved over to the phone, which sat on a small circular end table beside the entrance. He dialed the numbers on the rotary and heard the line connect after two rings.

"Hello?" the voice on the other end said, a groggy tone hanging about the words.

A smile tugged at Everette's lips upon hearing the sound of his friend's voice. "Red? Hi, it's Everette calling."

"Hey there, Everette. Did you get to the place okay?" There was a pause before Red added, "I was expecting you to call a little bit ago."

"Oh yeah, no issues at all. Beautiful drive, took my time to take it all in. You weren't kidding."

"I know, I say the same thing every year. Does everything look to be in order? No smashed windows or downed power lines or anything? I heard there was a big storm there last weekend."

"I just stepped in, but from the walk up the driveway I didn't see anything out of place or—"

"Good, good," Red interjected, sounding distracted.

Everette decided he would break the lull in the conversation by bringing up the task at hand. "Thanks again for letting me stay the week up here. I really needed the change of scenery. And of course, I'll winterize the place. You can count on me."

"Thank you again for doing it. The whole process should take maybe an afternoon max. Do that on your last day up there. Six and a half days of quiet lakeside views and chilly air." There was a pause and then, "I envy you."

"I'm looking forward to it for sure. Brought a few books and a couple beers, just something to take the edge off."

"Thanks again," Red replied, seeming to ignore the last sentence Everette had spoken. "With my back the way it is, I just can't do the drive to get up there right now, let alone doing all the winterizing. I'm afraid if I wait another month till my back is better, the pipes will freeze and ... well, I don't want to even think what the price tag would be to fix everything." There was a pause again and it sounded as if Red was stifling a yawn. "Say, did you remember to bring the list?"

"Yeah, I got it right in the bag here." Everette's eyes darted to the duffle on the couch before he returned his gaze to the window and the choppy sea outside.

"Good, good. I just didn't anticipate my back, you know? But still, take my advice: Get a drink, drag a chair out to the shore and just stare at the water as the sun sets. Nothing more relaxing in the entire world."

"It's the little things," Everette replied as he visualized Red's suggestion.

"It certainly is. Anyway, I'll let you go, so enjoy that sunset if the clouds aren't too heavy. Thanks again."

The line went dead with a click.

Everette was alone with his thoughts and the sounds of the lake that flowed through the window, the breeze fluttering the white curtains that hung in front of it. "It's just you and me," he said to the empty room.

He moved to the fridge and saw there were two beers sitting at the back. He grabbed one and pried off the cap with a bottle opener he found in the drawer. He tilted the bottle to his lips and felt the pressures of the week prior fade away as the beer entered his mouth. He let out a calming exhale and felt a sense of excitement at knowing he was on the outer cusp of his vacation and still had an entire week ahead of him.

Everette savoured the taste before deciding to explore the cabin in greater detail. He walked around the counter and moved back into the living room, his head turning to look into the first bedroom on his right. A closed suitcase sat on top of the bed. He raised an eyebrow and entered the room.

Red, you left your bag behind, he thought as he touched the black material. *His memory really is slipping these days,* Everette thought, reflecting how much older his friend and co-worker was. *I hope I'm not like that in twenty years.*

Everette took another sip of the beer, his mind turning to what Red had said about the car accident that had injured his back so terribly. He lingered on this thought for a while before shrugging and thinking, *I'll call him later in the week and see if he wants me to bring this bag home.*

Everette's fingers slipped away from the suitcase, but a

sense of curiosity got the better of him. He felt the steel of the zipper in his hand and before he knew it, he was opening the bag. The unzipping sound heightened, roaring through the cottage.

Everette tossed the flap aside and looked down to see a series of folded clothes. Long-sleeved shirts, jeans, balled up socks—nothing out of the ordinary. Still curious, he picked up a button-down shirt and marveled at the size. *A bit big for Red,* he thought as he tossed the shirt on top of the open suitcase.

Everette exited the room and walked two paces, peering into the second bedroom. This was clearly the smaller of the two, but still he nodded in satisfaction at the cozy nature of it. He pushed off from the door frame and moved through the living room and out the front door. The wind blew leaves across the wet grass, and he heard the waves swelling against the rocks on his right. The cold air nipped at his exposed skin, prompting him to zip up his jacket.

He unlocked his car and pulled out a case of beer from the back seat. He went to put the bottles down on the driveway, but frowned at how muddy it was. Finding a small collection of rocks, he placed the box down upon them, hearing the bottles clank as he did so. He looked down the road, admiring how the coloured leaves and spindly branches seemed to envelope the driveway, and by extension, the world beyond.

He returned his attention to his car and pulled a small grocery bag out from under the driver's seat. Inside was a leather toiletry bag. Giddy at just how alone he was, he unzipped the bag and admired the joints he had stored inside.

Everette knew full well what he would be doing when the sun set.

With a boyish grin on his face, he grabbed the case of beer and returned to the cabin with the toiletry bag carefully balanced on top. The sun was getting low in the sky, and he knew he had less than an hour until he could get his personal party started.

Everette placed half of the beers in the fridge before grabbing his luggage from the sofa and moving to the smaller bedroom. He had just tossed the bags on the bed and bent down to untie his shoes when the sound of something in the distance caused his ears to perk up.

An approaching engine.

He looked to the bedroom window and saw a pair of headlights moving through the gaps in the trees before coming around the bend. Everette watched through the blinds as an old Chevy pickup truck rolled up the remainder of the driveway and parked behind his car. A burly man with the beginnings of a greying beard exited the truck with some effort.

Who the hell is this? Everette thought as his pulse quickened. He could feel his fingers pulling the blinds farther apart to take in more of this intruder.

"Hello?" the stranger called out in a harsh voice as the wind began to pick up, blowing his unkempt thinning hair around. "Hello?" he repeated as he walked toward the cottage.

Everette moved to his luggage and retrieved a small knife from the front pocket. He thought of hiding the marijuana but ignored the notion as he moved out into the living room. He heard the stranger call out once more, but this time it was quieter as it came from the side of the cabin.

He gripped the closed knife in his right hand, eying the screen door as it banged against its frame from the wind coming off the lake. The stranger appeared and began to climb the creaking wooden steps.

Everette moved a pace forward. "Can I help you?" he asked. His voice was firm, a hint of annoyance lingering between the words.

The stranger's eyebrows furrowed and his head tilted back,

clearly offended. "Help *me?* Can I help you?" Then, his voice swelling into a bellow, "This is Redford Jennings' property! What are you doing here?"

"I know whose property it is," Everette snapped back. "I was invited here."

"Red never said nothing about that," the stranger said, climbing the remainder of the stairs with slow determination.

Everette gripped the knife tighter in his palm as the man approached. "Don't come in here!" he shouted, his voice becoming shaky as he moved toward the door to slam it shut.

Realizing what Everette meant to do, the stranger reached into his pocket and said, "You can lock it, but I have a key."

Everette's eyes darted between the man's thick face and his hand that held a silver key between thumb and forefinger.

"Where did you get that?" Everette's voice trembled all the more.

"Can I come in now?" the stranger asked.

"Where did you get that?' Everette repeated, his hand still wrapped around the edge of the door.

The man took a controlled breath. "Red gave it to me." He opened the screen door and Everette stepped back. "Like I said, I was invited here." The stranger took a step into the living room and said, "I should be asking you how you got in here. I know I locked the place tight when I left."

"I— Red gave me a key," Everette said, taking a step back toward the fireplace, his eyes still locked on the man.

"Right," the stranger replied as he moved into the kitchen. He placed his hand on the refrigerator and stopped, his eyes appearing to sear right through Everette. "You know what? I bet he invited the both of us up here to winterize the place." Seeing how Everette's face shifted into a confused expression prompted the man to add, "His memory is slipping a bit." He opened the fridge and removed one of the beers. Everette scowled as he watched the man pry off the lid and take an extended sip of the chilled beer.

"I'm gonna call him," Everette said, approaching the black rotary.

The man wiped his mouth with the back of his hand and said, "It won't do you any good. The phone lines are down."

Everette held the phone to his ear and dialed the first number, but realized there was no sound coming from the speaker. He lowered the phone to the cradle and stepped back toward the center of the room, his right hand shaking from the pressure he was putting on the hilt of the still folded knife. "How did you know that?"

In contrast, the stranger appeared quite relaxed, taking another sip of beer, hand still on the top of the fridge as he leaned against the slightly dented antique. "They've been down since I got here."

"No... Not possible." Everette shook his head. "I called Red not even twenty minutes ago."

Hearing this, the stranger took a step away from the fridge and placed his beer on the counter.

"Stay there!" Everette commanded, taking another step back.

"Easy there fella," the man said, eying Everette's right hand as he finally noticed the hilt of the weapon. His eyes lingered there for a moment before moving to Everette's sweating face. "Look, I just came from the next town over. They had a big windstorm in the afternoon; that's what blew the lines down." Seeing that Everette was not buying his explanation he added, "That's how I knew the phone wouldn't work."

"Prove you know Red then," Everette snapped.

The man sighed. "As I've been saying the whole time, I should be asking you to do that." He turned and moved back to the counter, hoisting the beer to his lips and mumbling, "Isn't it enough that I have a key?" He paused before adding, "But very well, I'll humor you. I met Red in elementary school, Grade Eight when he transferred in. Played high school football with him. He went to work at a factory job when he was eighteen. I was at both his weddings. He has three daughters, one with his ex-wife and two with his current one." He pointed a finger at Everette. "Now it's your turn. When's his birthday?"

Everette looked around the room, his mind lingering on the fact that this stranger had gotten all the prior information correct. "Um, twenty first... No, twenty second of June."

The man wrinkled his nose as if he was not expecting Everette to have known that. He took another sip, "And the names of his daughters?"

"Katie, Sarah..." Everette replied without hesitation, but quickly lost momentum coming up with the third name. *I didn't know Red had a daughter with his ex-wife,* he realized.

"Mary is the last one. The oldest," the stranger said. He raised his eyebrows in a disapproving manner before adding, "And how do you know Red?"

"I, uh, work with him. I met him when I started at K.W. Automotive something like ten years ago."

"I was gonna say, you look a fair bit younger than Red and I." The stranger paused, raising his chin toward the ceiling and let out a deep reverberating laugh. "That all checks out." He took a step toward the fridge. "And to think I doubted you." He opened it and retrieved a bottle, placing it on the counter. "Beer?"

Everette stepped toward the kitchen and mumbled a quick "thanks" before prying off the cap with the nearby bottle opener.

As he tasted the first sip, he realized that he already had an open beer sweating on the nightstand in the bedroom, but his mind left the thought behind when the stranger spoke again.

"The name's Art. Art Billings." He held out a mitt of a hand to shake.

"Everette," he replied, feeling his palm become swallowed up in the shake. As he retrieved his hand from the embrace he said, "So you really think he invited both of us up here and forgot? I know his mind is going a little with age, but..."

Art chuckled. "Wouldn't surprise me." He licked his teeth and added, "He invited me over for a poker game around this time last year and forgot the chips." He laughed again, which startled Everette. "I don't know if you've ever tried to play poker without chips, but it just isn't done. We tore his house apart trying to find them. Ended up using pennies instead."

"I think I was invited to that game," Everette said, feeling his nerves subside as he felt the beer settle in his stomach. "Couldn't go. My wife—well, ex-wife now—she had the flu."

Art smacked his lips. "That's rough. But it was a fun time. Just think, if you had come out to that game, we would have met before and avoided this little hostile meeting." He laughed again.

Everette smirked before something occurred to him. He lowered his beer to the counter, his eyes focused on the man's weathered features. "You said you went to the next town over, and that's how you knew the lines were down."

"Ya, I was getting supplies," Art said, his eyes narrowing. "Why?"

"Where are the supplies then?" Everette asked, pushing himself off from the counter, tension rising through him again.

"In the truck." Art rubbed his face for a moment. "Will you relax?" He raised his arm and threw a thumb over his shoulder in the direction of the driveway. "I saw your car and was going to investigate before I brought them in."

Everette slowly relaxed against the counter again, accepting the explanation and feeling a little foolish for jumping to the conclusion that this man was still trying to con him.

"Speaking of which," Art added as a nasty gust of wind reverberated off the windows, "I bought lots of stuff, including a tub of ice cream. Don't want it to melt." He placed the nearly empty beer bottle on the counter and wiped his palm on his faded jeans. "Here, come give me a hand with it."

"Why can't you go by yourself?" Everette asked as he felt for the hilt of the knife in his pocket.

Art shook his head, his unkempt hair shifting. "I could," he said patronizingly, "but it's a lot and I would appreciate a hand." His eyes flamed as he asked, "What's the matter with you?"

"I, uh— Well..."

"You going to help me or not?" Art asked as he moved from around the counter. His voice had lost any humor it had once contained.

Everette slowly moved from the counter and followed the man outside, his mind becoming lost on just how low the sun had gotten. The creaking hinges snapped his focus back to reality and he walked down the wooden steps and around the side of the cabin. The sounds of stones and mud underfoot echoed into the trees.

As they approached the truck, Art said, "To be honest, it's nice having a second pair of hands around when you winterize. We should be able to do everything in half the time." His voice sounded pleasant again and Everette wondered if this man was okay mentally or suffered from some sort of repressed anger issues.

Everette did not reply, instead thinking, *I was looking forward to being alone.*

Art opened his truck and pulled out a paper bag full of groceries from behind the driver's seat. Everette reached out to receive the bag, but his eyes wandered to the back window of the truck cab. A bolt action rifle hung there, mounted on a black rack. He heard a crash and looked down to see that the bag of groceries had fallen through his grasp.

Art spun around, his nostrils flaring. "What are you doing? You had your hands out—" He straightened up, his loud breathing sending a chill down Everette's spine. "At least that one didn't have the eggs in it." He bent back down into the truck, mumbling profanities under his breath.

Everette lowered himself and picked up the paper bag, hardly aware that he had done so as his mind stayed focused on the rifle. He still didn't trust this man, and he certainly didn't trust him enough to have such easy access to a firearm. As he stood up, he nodded to Art in an attempt to offer a vague apology.

"Told you it was a lot," Art said in an effort to try and break the tension as he hoisted two additional bags of his own, shutting the truck door with his back.

Everette again stayed quiet and followed Art back to the cottage, his mind returning to the firearm. He was so focused on it he hardly heard Art say, "Beautiful night," over the sound of the violent waters just ahead.

Everette followed Art's gaze as he stopped to admire the last rays of sunlight that hung over the trees jutting up from the coastline to the west. "Yeah, it's great," Everette said in a dismissive tone, his face turning sour. He couldn't believe he would have to share the cabin with someone who talked as much as Art seemed to.

Mundane conversation. A waste of time. It's only for people who like the sound of their own voice, he thought, the crinkling of the paper bag becoming louder as he tightened his arm around it.

Art resumed his pace and trudged up the steps. He pulled

open the screen door and moved into the cabin, placing the groceries on the counter. He retrieved several items from the bag before reaching in and revealing a tub of ice cream. He hoisted it proudly, saying, "It's Rocky Road. The best as far as I'm concerned." He placed it in the freezer and asked, "So what's your story?"

"Me? I don't have much of one to tell." Everette's tone reverberated with disinterest.

"You must have a story. Friends of Red are always interesting people. Wife, kids? You hunt?"

"What? Uh, no. I—"

"Oh ya, you said you were divorced. Kids, then?"

"No, my wife didn't want any. She was a piece of work. Still is, I guess."

"Ex-wives usually are," Art replied, a sliver of a smile tugging at his lips.

"And yourself? Kids?" Everette struggled to keep the conversation going.

"Two sons. We all hunt together, fish together. You know, father-son trips."

"Oh," Everette replied in little more than a grunt as he handed Art several items from the grocery bags.

"Nothing else for the fridge, everything else can stay out," Art said before offering a soft smile and moving into the larger of the two bedrooms.

Everette took a deep breath, hoping he would be alone now, and that the incessant conversation would cease.

"Hey!" Art called out, agitation clear in his voice. He appeared back in the door frame with the shirt Everette had tossed aside in one hand. "What's the big idea, going through a man's stuff?"

"I thought it was Red's! I—"

"You throw other people's things around wherever you like

then?" Art questioned, his eyes staying locked on Everette's thin face.

"I didn't mean to. I-I just... I thought I was alone and I..." Everette stammered, his pulse thundering in his neck.

Art opened his mouth to speak, but nothing came out. A moment passed and it appeared that he was forcing himself to swallow his agitation. "Don't touch my stuff," Art said in a firm tone that boomed with authority.

"I'm sorry. I won't," Everette said, but his mind had already shifted to the rifle mounted in the truck.

Art lowered the shirt and seemed to take several calming breaths. "No use yelling about it, I suppose. I know you didn't take anything, but at first that's what I thought when I..." He trailed off, moving into the kitchen and pulling open the fridge door. "Here, I'll open another beer and all will be forgiven."

Why do I feel like it won't be? Everette thought.

The chatter of jangling bottles accompanied the sound of the fridge door shutting with more force than necessary.

Everette awoke, eyes wide and skin crawling.

Someone's on the porch, he thought as he lifted his head and searched the dark room. The clothing hanging in the open closet played tricks on his eyes, the sleeves of the garments twisting into haunting spectres.

He took a deep breath in an attempt to calm himself and tried to listen to the sounds of the cabin. Art's snoring from the next room drowned out all other sounds. Everette looked to the wall on his left, as if he could see into the room and will Art to cease the incessant racket.

It was his damn snoring that woke me up—

The sound of creaking from outside his room caused his

head to bolt forward. Everette's eyes fixated on the closed door. A series of footfalls thumped around outside. His pulse thundered in his ears.

Who is that? he wondered, his limbs taking on a life on their own as they began to tremble.

The footfalls continued and Everette deduced by the sound of creaking wood that this person must be on the porch. He looked around the room for a flashlight, a book of matches, something, *anything* to help calm his nerves. He saw his pocket knife on the dresser. With a quick lunge he seized it and stood slowly.

Art's snoring continued to reverberate through the walls, but still the footsteps continued, almost as if they were purposely paced so he could hear them. Everette approached the door with care, attempting to be as silent as he could. As his hand touched the handle, the footfalls ceased.

Everette thought he might die of fright in that moment, as the uncertainty of what might befall him put his imagination into overdrive. Images of an axe wielding madman staring through the living room window; red eyes and a twisted, all-knowing smile.

He took a moment to collect himself, trying to rationalize that it was the wind he was hearing, and the footsteps were a coincidence. As he began to turn the handle, he heard the footfalls move off from the porch at a quickened pace.

Everette threw open the door, his eyes scanning the living room. He listened for the sounds in between Art's bellowing snores and moved his gaze to the window over the kitchen sink. He saw a flash of movement and recognized it was the top of someone's head as they moved past the window.

He stepped forward. The thought of charging into the night to apprehend this intruder seemed reasonable, almost a sure thing, until he thought better of it.

That's what they want me to do. They want me to follow them.

He moved over to the kitchen window, craning his neck in an attempt to look out and get another glimpse of the person, but all he could see was the muddy driveway.

Everette turned around and threw on the light to the kitchen. He wanted to let the intruders know he was awake. He moved into the living room and did the same.

Art's snoring broke off and he heard a mumbled, "Huh? What? Who's there?" from behind his ajar bedroom door.

Everette hardly heard him as he now stood between the white curtain and the living room window, his eyes focused on the shoreline.

"Everette?" Art asked, now sitting up in bed. "That you?"

"There's someone outside," Everette replied, his eyes locked on the crashing waves.

"What?" Art snapped in a stern whisper. He was up in a flash. He walked up beside Everette, his eyes scanning the door, then drifting toward the kitchen. "How many? Did they try to get in?"

Everette shook his head, the knife growing slippery in his palm. "Go get your gun," he whispered after a moment.

"My... My rifle? Now?" Art asked, staring at the spot in the curtain where Everette stood behind. "I ain't going out there!"

"But what if they try to get in?" Everette asked, licking his dry lips.

Art reached toward the door handle and checked to see if it was locked. It was. Satisfied, he turned and drew back the curtain from Everette. As he did so, he asked, "What did you see exactly?"

"A person by that window." He pointed toward the window overlooking the sink. Art took two strides toward the kitchen before Everette added, "But I heard them on the porch first."

Art stuck his head to the glass, looking as best he could down the driveway, his breath fogging up the glass. "No one there now. You think it was kids or—"

"Let's get your gun," Everette said, moving away from the large window.

"No. The easiest way for them to get in is when you go out. Not to mention it's a sure-fire way to get killed. All my cop buddies agree on that."

"How many is that?" Everette asked, taking a step toward the kitchen.

"How many is what?" Art replied, his voice carrying a tone of annoyance. He left the kitchen window and turned around to face Everette.

"How many cop friends do you have?"

Art moved past him and entered his bedroom. "Enough," he said over his shoulder, as he separated the closed blinds with his finger so he could peer through the slit unhindered. "Our cars are still there. No windows broken from what I can see. Probably just bored teenagers that wandered up from the beach somewhere."

Beach? What beach? Everette thought as fiddled with the knife in his hand. *It's all rock. There needs to be sand for it to be a beach...*

He kept this thought to himself and stepped toward the living room window. He pulled the curtain aside and looked out toward the lake. A silver fog hung over the water, slowly blowing inland. It would envelope the cottage within the hour.

Chapter 2

Tossed in the Deep End

Art woke to the sounds of birds chirping in the distance. The daze of sleep still clung to him as he rolled over and a grunt escaped his lips. A hand flew to his lower back and he groaned as he sat up, pain shooting up his spine.

What is this mattress made out of? I've slept on dirt floors that were more comfortable.

He let his hand drop from his back and looked around the room. Soft morning light shone through the slits in the blinds, coating the room in an orange hue. Tugging at his beard, he climbed out of bed with a grimace, feeling several joints click and pop as he did. He twisted the rod attached to the blinds and let the fresh light enter the room unhindered. Admiring the parked vehicles, he nodded with satisfaction at their presence.

He turned, picking up his watch from the bedside table, and squinted to see the time. *A quarter to nine,* he thought as he looked out the window again, eyeing Everette's grey sedan. He didn't know why but he couldn't shake the feeling that he didn't fully trust Everette. *There's just something about him,* his inner voice called out from the deep recesses of his mind, as his hand tightened the watch band around his wrist.

Art moved out into the living room and looked at the closed door to Everette's room. *Did he actually see someone last night?* He unconsciously licked his lips as he weighed both sides of the thought. *He was very eager for me to get my gun.*

He turned his attention away from the door and moved toward the kitchen. He could smell the early morning dew coming through the open window as his eyes studied the collection of long emptied beer bottles. He picked up a bottle and looked at the torn label on it, immediately identifying that it must have been Everette's drink. Art returned the bottle to its spot on the counter.

Why would he make something like that up? I must be all wrong about the guy. He loosened up once he had a few drinks in him. It's just because we got off on the wrong foot and I'm not giving him a fair shake.

Art pivoted and opened the cabinet closest to him. He retrieved a fresh filter and a tin of ground coffee. After filling the reservoir with water, he switched on the maker. As he grabbed a *Reagan-Bush 84* mug from the cabinet he thought, *The little fella doesn't drink too much though.* His eyes returned to the assembly of empty bottles. *Maybe I should follow his example. Why can I never have just one?*

The door to Everette's room opened over the sounds of the coffee maker grumbling to life. Everette moved into the living room, his eyes hardly more than slits as he looked hatefully toward the light that filled the room.

"Morning," Art said with a neutral expression on his face.

Everette grunted a response, rubbing his arms. "It's cold in here." He pivoted and returned to the bedroom.

Art waited for the coffee to brew and proceeded to pour some into his mug. He added a spoonful of sugar before moving into the living room and looking out of the window to marvel at the crystalline lake. Even through the thin curtains he could see how blue the water appeared. "Oh, how I love the sea."

"Sea?" Everette asked, his voice was far from friendly as he approached from behind. "It's a lake. It isn't a sea."

Art fought himself from sighing. "Due to their size, the Great Lakes can be considered inland seas. Doesn't matter if they're connected to the ocean or not."

"That's the stupidest definition I've ever heard."

"Don't argue with me; argue with the encyclopedia," Art offered as a curt reply. He could see Everette peering through the curtain as well. After a long delay, Art cleared his throat and said for the sake of conversation, "Crazy to think it will be snowing in just a few weeks."

"Or freezing rain," Everette mumbled.

"Right," Art said as he turned, his eyes focusing on the sweater Everette wore. "You went to Florida State?" Art asked, gesturing at the logo on Everette's sweater. He sipped his coffee before adding, "My brother went there. Well, he's not really my brother ... he's a cousin, but we were close like brothers."

Everette looked down at the sweater for a moment before returning his gaze to the window. "No, I didn't. It's a friend of... It's my wife's, actually. It was always big on her."

"She let you keep it in the divorce?" Art questioned, perplexed.

"She left it behind," Everette replied before his eyes darted to Art's mug. "You made coffee?"

"Ya, a whole pot. I drink a lot of the stuff." He smiled a big toothy grin before adding, "I always have a pot brewing."

Everette clicked his tongue once before moving into the kitchen. Art watched as he poured himself a mug before adding, "If it were me, I would have burned it."

"What? The coffee?" Everette asked, not taking his eyes from the pot. "I don't smell anything."

"No, the sweater. When me and my wife split up, I didn't keep a single damn thing as a reminder." He paused, shaking his head as he did so. "Well, except my sons, of course. I'd keep them, flesh and blood and all that, but we have shared custody. To be honest though Rick can be moody sometimes, so maybe I would let her keep that one full time." He laughed. "I joke, of course. I love my boys. Early teens now, the two of them."

"Did you buy sugar?" Everette asked as he rummaged through a trio of cabinets.

"Yeah, I put it next to the toaster. That bag there," Art replied, pointing vaguely. He frowned, feeling that Everette was not appreciating the multiple chances to continue the conversation he had been lobbing toward him.

Everette shoveled several spoonful's worth of sugar into his mug, stirring it gingerly with a spoon he had grabbed from a drawer. The cabin filled with relative silence, which made Art uneasy. To break the tension he asked, "So you ever play ball? High school or college level, I mean?"

"No," Everette offered as a curt response.

"Really? Because if you could catch you got the build for a wide receiver or maybe—"

Everette rolled his eyes before letting his spoon drop into his mug, his face showing contempt. "Look, I'm going to be honest."

"I hate that," Art replied quickly, knowing where this was going.

"What?" Everette snapped back. He placed the mug on the counter and folded his arms. "Honesty?"

"No, people who say, 'I'm going to be honest.' It's like everything you've said before was *dishonest*," Art replied with an exasperated breath. "Anyway, what? Let me have it. You seem annoyed by my presence."

Everette licked his teeth, his eyes appearing to study the ceiling, searching for the correct way to proceed. "No. Well ... yes, I am. You seem nice, but I was looking forward to my alone time."

"And you don't think I was looking forward to the same?" Art barked as he moved from the window. "Of course, I wanted to be alone. I had plans—day drinking, some bonfires, I got the new Edgar Grissom novel and I heard it's good. But..." He tried to lighten the mood with a smile. "I'm making the best of it. Trying to be cordial. A 'nice guy,' as you put it. By getting to know each other, maybe we can both have a good time."

"Okay," Everette replied before shaking his head and raising the mug to his lips.

Art stared at him, feeling the heat of anger rising up inside him. *This guy is the biggest asshole I've ever met.*

Everette cleared his throat before saying, "I'll try to engage in conversation more." There was a long pause and then, "I'm just not a talker. But I appreciate you trying to be ... friendly. I-I'll get used to it." The last few words sounded like it pained him to utter them.

Art felt his glare loosen. "Alright," he replied, and moved over to the kitchen counter, arms wide. "And if I'm being annoying, you just let me know."

Everette nodded slightly and Art figured that was the best reply he was going to get. He placed his mug on the counter before clapping his hands together. "I'm going to head into town in a minute."

Everette's eyes took on a peculiar look as he asked, "Why?" He sipped his drink and regained his composure. "You were just there."

"I'm going to the drugstore. Gotta get some anti-inflammatory cream or some aspirin or something. My back is killing me from sleeping on that slab of a mattress."

"Really? My bed's fine," Everette replied, then looked down at the contents of his mug.

"I'm sure it is," Art said as he rubbed his lower back. "You want to come as well? You need anything?"

"What? Um, no. No, I'm good ... thanks. I'm okay here." Everette's voice had taken on a mousey tone.

"You sure? It would get you out of the house? Probably get into town by, say, nine forty-five, maybe ten if we get stuck behind a truck. We could get some breakfast."

"No, I'm good here," Everette replied, a bite clinging to his words. He forcibly lightened his tone as he added, "I want to enjoy my morning. I got stuff I want to do."

"Oh? What do you want to get done?" Art asked. "You're on vacation."

"I want to finish this coffee," Everette replied, taking a sip. The disdain in his voice was unmistakable.

Art crossed the street toward the pay phone that sat next to a shabby old bar. He looked down the road as a relic of an automobile turned a corner where a diner sat comfortably at the end of the block. Seeing the restaurant brought the idea of eggs and bacon to the forefront of Art's mind. He nodded to himself at the prospect and entered the phone booth.

He inserted a quarter and asked the operator for the number to call Redford Jennings. The operator complied and the line began to ring.

"Hello?" Red's voice sounded through the speaker after the third ring.

"Red? It's Art. I'm calling from the town here."

"Town? What town?" Red's voice sounded overly aggravated.

"Heartford Meadow," Art replied as he turned in the booth, looking down the road at the various businesses that served the small downtown sector.

"Oh, that one." Red sounded confused but continued anyway, "Yes, good little town. How you doing, Art? You didn't call last night to tell me you made it up there okay."

"I tried but the lines were down. Some big windstorm they kept talking about." He adjusted his grip on the phone. "But Everette said he called you last night. I guess they got it working for a short while. Do you remember inviting both of us up here?" Art asked. His tone was more accusatory than he would have liked.

"Everette? Up there?" Red replied after a brief pause. "I-I don't know. Hmm..." Silence filled the speaker for several moments until he added, "Oh, shoot. I did invite him. Oh, I'm sorry, Art. Did I ruin your getaway? I invited him that week you said you couldn't do it, something about your fishing trip..."

"Right, but when that fell through, I said I could do it."

"Right. *Right.*" Red sounded annoyed with himself. "I must have forgotten that I told Everette he could go..." He paused. "Damn my memory! I gave him a key one day at work and everything."

"I don't mind. Really, I'm fine. But I'm surprised you're so taken aback by this; he said he called you last night."

"No one called me last night," Red replied, the sound of frustration still clear in his voice.

"No? Well, he said he did."

"No one called here."

"Alright, but... Well, I mean this as a friend when I ask: Would you remember? Fully, I mean."

"No one called here!" Red snapped. "I can tell you what I did last night down to the minute. I ain't heard from Everette since work on Friday." There was a noise that sounded like he hit a table with his palm. "I should have remembered that I invited both of you, I'm sorry. I had even written him a list and everything."

"Don't mention it. It's okay, really. It's fine. I was just calling to check in. But say, did you just mention that you haven't seen Everette since Friday? As in yesterday?"

"No, last Friday I said. Like a week ago. He took the week off sick." There was a pause. "That's why I forgot about him and double booked and—"

"Well, he looks fine now," Art said absentmindedly. "Listen, Red, I'm gonna let you go. But rest assured we will get the property winterized just the way you like it."

"Good to hear from you. Tell Everette sorry for the double booking. I'll have you all over for steaks and cards when you get back. I'll remember the poker chips this time..." There was a laugh and then, "Yeah, the six of us will have a great time."

"Six?" Art asked, doing some quick math on his free hand. "Who's the sixth person?"

"You and your new lady friend, Margery and me, and Everette and his wife Tammy. Six of us."

"He said he's divorced," Art replied as he watched a rusted truck splash a funnel of water from a pothole onto the overgrown grass.

"Oh, that's a shame. News to me. He never mentioned it."

"Well, Red, I'll let you go. But I'll be taking you up on the steaks."

They said their goodbyes once more before Art hung up the phone. He heard the quarter slip down into the machine and exited the booth. He felt several raindrops land on his forehead as he moved back across the street, thinking, *Man, Red's memory really is slipping.*

Art parked his truck, grabbed the small bag of goods he had purchased from the pharmacy and started his trek up the driveway. Within a few paces he noticed several shoe prints in the mud leading to and from Everette's car. It looked like multiple trips had taken place.

Same shoe prints though, Art thought as he stopped and studied them for a moment. *Someone* was *outside last night. Everette wasn't lying.* He straightened up, scratched his forehead and continued past the car. *Then again, those could be Everette's shoe prints from the day prior.*

He moved along the side of the cabin, feeling a faint spray of lake mist as the waves stirred in angry might. He walked up the steps to the porch and opened the door.

Everette was sitting on the couch, book in hand. He was breathing heavily, but appeared to be trying to mask it. As Art moved into the kitchen Everette lowered the tattered paperback and asked, "Got everything you need?"

"Ya, already put some cream on in town. My back was killing me." He turned and watched as Everette wiped perspiration from his forehead. "Say, are you okay?"

"Why?" Everette responded, raising the book to his eye level again.

"You're sweating and breathing heavily." Art cocked his head as he noticed Everette had mud around the cuffs of his jeans. Art's gaze gravitated to the shoes by the door and noticed they were muddy as well.

"I was exercising," Everette replied after a moment. He

lowered the book with exasperation and sniffed the air, letting out a deep sigh in the process.

"In jeans?" Art questioned, his eyes narrowing with disappointment at what he perceived as such an obviously false statement.

"I didn't bring any workout clothes. Besides, it was just a few push-ups."

"I see," Art said, his mind again moving to the muddy shoes by the entrance. He blinked once before spinning around and opening the fridge door. While his eyes moved like he was searching for something, his mind was focused on other matters.

So what if the shoe prints belong to Everette? It's his car, he can go near it as much as he likes. He might have had another bag in there or something. I really have to be more trusting. He pulled out a stick of butter and a carton of eggs. *Maybe he just went for a walk or took out the garbage or something.*

He could see the trash container in his peripherals. The items from yesterday evening were still inside.

"I'm making eggs. Do you want any? I can put on some bacon too."

"No, I already ate," Everette replied as he flipped a page in the book. "Thank you."

"Oh," Art said as a curt response. He cracked an egg open and spilled its contents into the rapidly heating pan.

He gritted his teeth and thought, *I knew I should have just eaten at that restaurant.* He cracked another egg into the pan as his mind returned to the presence of his unwanted companion that he was forced to bear for the week ahead. *I don't know what it is, but I just don't trust this guy.*

Everette bolted up again. He heard it plain as day.

"Everette," the voice whispered. "Everette..."

He scanned the dark room. No one was there. But that voice, oh God, how that summoning call had sliced through his dreams and shackled him to the dreary world. A chill of sweat moved over his body as he got to his feet. The wind howled outside, causing the branches of the forest to creak and groan.

"Everette," the voice called again from somewhere in the distance.

He swallowed as he grabbed the pocket knife from the bedside table. He pulled out the blade, admiring how it picked up the moonlight through the slit in the blinds.

"Everette..."

He moved across the room and threw open the door. The living room was calm, everything where it had been when he had retired to bed earlier in the night.

"Everette."

He looked to the left and screamed at what he saw there.

A pale face hovered in the kitchen window. A pair of crazed brown eyes beaming into his soul.

Art bounded into the room, rifle in hand, his gaze affixed on the trembling Everette.

The figure pivoted and disappeared from view as it headed toward the parked vehicles.

"What? Are they back?" Art yelled as he swung the rifle around in the direction of Everette's shocked stare.

"I saw it," Everette replied, his voice a jittering mess. "It was ... the same person."

Art moved to the kitchen window and looked down the driveway in a similar fashion as the night prior. Seeing no signs of movement, he looked into the woods beside the cabin and asked, "How do you know it was the same person?"

"It was the same person. I know it was!" Everette snapped.

With a determined pace, Art returned to his room, the sling of his rifle jangling as he moved to the window and raised the blinds with his free hand.

"No one there," he announced after his eyes completed one scan of the yard. He turned to face Everette, who was still frozen in place in the living room. "No one there," he repeated, his voice quieter this time. "But how could you see someone through the kitchen window? They would have to be at least eight feet tall to see in."

"Look, I saw someone, okay?" Everette replied as he plopped down onto the sofa and began to open and close the blade of his knife repeatedly.

"I believe you. I never said I didn't," Art said, lowering the blinds. "I was just asking a question."

"It was your tone," Everette mumbled.

"My tone?" Art replied, placing the rifle on the bed and moving out into the living room.

"Ya, your tone, and the whole, 'No one there.' Like you're accusing me of making it up."

"I never said you did. My tone is the same as it has always been." Art was now standing tall over the sitting Everette. "It's just you're the only one to have seen this person, or group or whatever. I never have."

"There it is," Everette said, throwing up his hands. "I knew you didn't believe me. Maybe if you left your gun with me like I wanted I could have shot the person, then we would have a body and I could prove it." He began to ground his teeth. "Is that what you want, a body? I can arrange it," he snarled.

"We aren't shooting anyone, not unless they actually get in. And even then, I ain't going to jail for clipping some unarmed home invader. This ain't a castle state."

"Let's call the cops. Maybe they can get this person, have

'em in a line up by morning. Then you would believe me, wouldn't you?" Everette was frantic now.

"Look, I believe you," Art's voice was stern, but as he spoke his tone softened. "But calling the local P.D. won't do any good. By the time they get out here, this person will be long gone. If the cops even bother to come before sun-up, that is."

Everette's eyes turned hateful. "You don't know that."

"I do know that," Art retorted, looking over his shoulder to the kitchen window. "Small outfits like this keep one, *maybe* two officers on standby and we would literally be waking these people up. Unless someone is dead or there are gunshots, they aren't coming before sun-up."

"Oh yeah? How do you know so much?" Everette's voice had a biting edge to it as he stood up, his hands balled into fists.

"Because I was one for twenty years. I know how different forces operate and I know trespasser types; they run off at the first sign of trouble. Unless they were actually trying to harm us, that's different."

"Y-you're police?" Everette stuttered.

"*Was* police. Retired."

"Retired or fired?" Everette asked, his eyes searching Art's face as if the answer would appear upon it.

"Retired. Some fuc—" Art closed his eyes for a moment before softening his tone. "Some *guy* shot me in the shoulder, robbed me of the last bit of my career."

"You were shot?" Everette's eyes moved to where Art's finger indicated.

"Yup. Guy is still in prison too, last I heard. Murdered his wife, resisted arrest, attempted murder of a P.O. Guy got life. *Trifecta of crime* the paper called it."

"Sounds like a degenerate piece of shit," Everette retorted, taking a sudden seat on the couch, rubbing his hands against his thighs.

"By all accounts his wife was a lovely woman."

"I hate the crazies," Everette replied before standing abruptly, his eyes moving around the cabin. He shook his head before returning to his room, slamming the door behind him.

Art eyed the sofa where Everette had just been. *Yeah, the crazies*, he thought as he moved over to the living room window. The wind had died down and the water had begun to even out.

Chapter 3

An Irresistible Current

Art drove past the restaurant in town. His excuse of needing to run to the store again to buy stronger pain relief medication had seemingly worked on Everette, who hadn't asked any follow-up questions. As Art recalled, Everette had actually lit up and said, "That will give me some time to myself."

Perfect, Art thought as he saw the sheriff's car sitting in the restaurant parking lot.

He turned the corner and entered the gravel lot before exiting his truck and entering the restaurant. A bell rang overhead as he did so. The restaurant was more crowded than he had initially expected, but as his eyes passed over the various patrons, he recalled that it was a Sunday afternoon. A group of elderly people to his left looked up at him from their seats before returning to their mundane conversation.

A waitress approached in a yellow dress and apron, her hair tied up in a lackadaisical bun. "Table for one, hun?" she asked, grabbing a menu from the counter.

"Ya," Art replied as he looked to the right of the restaurant and saw the sheriff sitting alone in a booth.

While the officer sat facing the door, his eyes studied the newspaper in front of him.

"Can I get that table?" Art asked as the waitress motioned him forward. He pointed to the empty spot beside the sheriff.

"Sure thing, sweetheart," she replied and guided him to the table of his choosing. "Coffee?" she asked as he sat down.

"Sure, that sounds good," Art said absentmindedly as his eyes shot toward the sheriff. He was attempting to gauge if this man had a good head on his shoulders or would be beyond lazy due to the simplicity of small-town policing.

"Our special today is a BLT, home fries and a side of soup," the waitress added before leaving, but Art had hardly heard her. Instead he kept his eyes on the sheriff who took a sip of coffee.

Art slid out of his booth and stood over the sheriff's table, a soft smile etched on his face to appear less threatening. "Morning, Sheriff," Art said after a moment when the officer didn't look up.

The sheriff took his eye from the paper and replied, "Morning." Upon realizing he didn't recognize Art, he added, "You need something?"

Art tugged at his beard. "Mind if I sit?"

The sheriff rubbed a hand up the back of his blonde crew cut. "Well, I was about to head back to the station—"

"This will be quick," Art said, prompting the sheriff to give a noncommittal shrug before gesturing to the seat across from him.

Art sat down just as the waitress came by with his coffee. Art motioned that he would take it at the sheriff's table before saying, "Sheriff, you don't know me, but I'm a friend of Red Jennings."

"Oh yeah? No kidding. How is Red doing? I didn't see him at all this past summer."

"He's fine, Sheriff. His memory is going a bit and he hurt his back in a fender bender, but still going strong."

"He's a funny guy, that Red," the sheriff said as he pushed his paper to the side. "So, what can I do for a friend of old Redford?"

"Well, here's the thing..." Art took a sugar packet from the small bowl and added the contents to his coffee. "I used to be a police officer myself and wanted to bounce something off you."

"Retired or..." the sheriff began, his eyes revealing that his interest was piqued.

"Ya, retired."

"What service?" the sheriff asked before gesturing to the waitress for more coffee.

"State Grass P.D. Just a small local outfit."

"Hey, nothing wrong with that." The sheriff chuckled as he looked around the diner. "Sometimes small-town local is the most rewarding. My brother is Chicago P.D. and he hates it. It's all park rummies, stabbings, domestics, B and Es." He paused, smiling at the waitress as she filled up his cup before continuing. "But he wanted to be the big man, go out into the world, leave little Heartford Meadow behind."

"Right. So listen, Sheriff, I like to think I'm a good judge of character and have a good sense of people, you know?" Art said. The sheriff nodded and opened a small container of milk before stirring it into his coffee. "And I'm staying at Red's cabin with a supposed friend of his. But this guy ... there's something about him that gives me the creeps."

"So, kick him out." The sheriff chuckled. "Or remove yourself from the situation."

"Yeah, I guess. But I don't know, I was hoping you could talk some sense into me, tell me I'm crazy or..."

"What's this fella been doing to rub you the wrong way?"

"Well, he keeps saying he sees people, like trespassers at night."

"At Red's place? Pretty far out in the sticks. No one around for easily a half mile. But maybe it's one of the neighbors from around the lake out for a stroll?"

"I don't think so. This is always in the middle of the night, and he says they come right up to the cabin. But the thing is, every time I get up and look, I don't see anyone. That's twice in a row, two nights." He held up two fingers to deliver the point home.

"Ready to order?" the waitress asked, causing Art to jump and knock the table in the process. The coffee in the mugs sloshed around inside their porcelain prisons.

"Uh, yeah, get me the special please," Art said quickly, turning his attention back to the sheriff.

"What kind of toast?" the waitress asked, her pen scribbling on a notepad.

"Brown's good," he replied in haste, before returning to his previous thought. "And that ain't the only thing neither. He—"

"What type of soup?" The waitress asked, glancing up from her idle pen. "We have cream of broccoli, Italian wedding, chicken noodle, tomato—"

"The first one," Art replied, his voice still pleasant but dangerously close to becoming short.

The sheriff's eyes followed the waitress as she walked away before he asked, "What sort of other stuff is this guy doing?"

"Well, nothing too odd on its own, but when you put it together... For example, he went through my stuff."

"Your stuff?" The sheriff screwed up his face. "Why'd he do that?"

"I don't know. He said he thought it was Red's and I guess that makes sense because he didn't know someone else would be staying there. See, Red invited the two of us by accident to winterize, but like I said, his memory is slipping."

"Why would he go through someone else's stuff?"

"I guess that's just the kind of guy he is," Art replied, trying to move past that point. "That's not all though. He just keeps giving me these weird looks. I mean, I guess he's not a people person but ... he's got one of those faces."

"Which kind?"

"One of those where if you saw this guy on the street you would think, *Oh that guy's got a criminal record for sure.* One of those guys you might want to ask a few additional questions to, you know?"

"Hmm?" the sheriff replied, his eyes starting to drift back to the paper. "So, this guy threaten you or something?"

"No, no, nothing like that. He kept asking for my hunting rifle though."

The sheriff's eyes moved back to Art's face. "What?"

"Ya, for the intruder or trespassers or whatever, but I don't trust this guy with a gun."

"Okay, so what do you need from me? You want me to talk with him or...?"

"No, I got that covered. I can still interview people." Art let out a slight chuckle. "But I was hoping you could run him." The sheriff raised an eyebrow and Art continued, "I know you aren't supposed to run people unless you are dealing with them or investigating them but I—"

"Why would me running his name in the database do anything for you?" the sheriff asked, his brow still wrinkled.

"Peace of mind for one thing," Art said, but phrased it more as a question. "I'm telling you, there's something off about him."

"Why not call your buddies at State Hill P.D. or wherever. Have them do it."

"I was just about to." He gestured over his shoulder toward

the phone booth down the street. "But I saw you parked here and figured I might as well ask." The sheriff stayed stone faced and Art continued, "You can call State Grass P.D. and verify I am who I say I am. Art Billings, retired in ninety. Badge number was zero eight five."

The sheriff pulled a notebook from his pocket and gave his pen a click. "Maybe I will." He looked up and asked, "Zero...?"

"Eight five. Art Billings."

"Alright, I got it," the sheriff replied, closing his notebook and leaving it next to the morning paper.

"Ask for a Lieutenant Rodgers and if he isn't in, then Sergeant Meford should be there. Guy never takes a day off. Loves the overtime. It's been a few years since I've seen them, but I know they didn't retire."

"Oh, one of those types, eh?" the sheriff mumbled as he reopened his notebook and jotted down the names. He looked up. "All right. I'll verify who you are when I get back to the station and if it all checks out I'll run this fella in the system and—"

"I was hoping you could run him from your cruiser computer."

"Cruiser computer? We don't have that here. This ain't New York," the sheriff replied before slurping his coffee. "The town barely gives me enough funds for road cones or new handcuffs. Where am I supposed to find the budget for a computer in my car?"

"Well, no, I guess not, But I figured—"

"You've only been retired, what, five and a half, six years? How far do you think technology has come since then? Those things are expensive, stupidly so. You think the mayor is gonna just give me one of those?" He laughed for a second and then added, "Did State Grass have them in their cruisers?"

"No... But I don't know, I guess I wasn't thinking."

"Anyways. I'll go to the station and do my checks. Say, you got a name for this guy?"

"Oh yeah, that would be important, wouldn't it?" Art replied with a quick smile on his face, but the sheriff's visage held a stern glisten. "Everette Davis. Late 30s, maybe early 40s, born in May. I got him to tell me that when I asked for his star sign and purposely got the month wrong. Pretty clever, eh?"

"Ya, I guess. Anything else? A year of birth would really help me."

"No, sorry. Brown hair, grey eyes, Caucasian. No tattoos on his arms that I could see."

The sheriff scribbled down another note. "All right, I'll see what I can do. You want me to call Red's place when I find out if he's got a past?"

"Um, no. Everette might answer. That would set him off. He got really weird when he found out I used to be a cop. That's what got my mind rolling on the criminal record idea. That, and the overall strangeness of him."

"So, you got another number I can reach you at?"

"No, but tell you what, how about I swing by the station tomorrow at around ten?"

The sheriff shrugged. "If it's ten, then you might as well meet me here. I always get coffee here." He tucked his notebook into his pocket and stood up. He reached for his wallet and said, "So why'd you retire? Sick of it, or..."

"I was shot."

The sheriff's eyes widened, head tilting. "I'm sorry to hear that. Well, I'm glad you're okay." The sheriff patted the revolver on his hip. "I've never had to fire this thing outside of the range. Hopefully I'll never have to." He placed a pair of one-dollar bills on the table before returning his wallet to his back pocket and walking toward the exit.

"I never fired mine neither," Art replied softly, but the

sheriff was already gone. The waitress moved toward his booth with a plate of food in one hand and a bowl of soup in the other.

Art heard the clicking of his blinker as he turned down the driveway of the property. He felt the bumping of gravel and heard the splash of a mud puddle as the truck passed over it. His eyes caught a flash of movement through the low hanging branches of the woods. A man dressed in jeans and a grey T-shirt was sprinting toward the cabin. In an instant, the figure was around the far corner of the house and out of sight.

Art felt his pulse quicken as his grip tightened around the steering wheel.

At first, he thought it must be one of the mysterious trespassers that Everette had reported the last two nights, but as he replayed the memory in his mind, he recognized that the figure he had just seen must have been Everette.

He looked in the direction his housemate had been running from, a small path in the trees sandwiched between a ratty shed and a pile of rotting firewood.

What's back there? he wondered as he brought his truck to a stop behind the familiar sedan. Art exited the vehicle and moved past Everette's car. *Was he running because he heard my truck? I have to be careful about this. To ask him directly would give away that I saw him running...*

He stopped in his tracks as his eyes picked up more footprints that had appeared around Everette's car. His eyes followed them as they collected around the trunk of the sedan before moving off of the driveway and into the uncut grass. Art bit his lip, knowing that the number of tracks had doubled since he had first noticed them yesterday.

Art looked at the calm cottage, eyeing the bedroom windows carefully. He knew he was being watched.

Just get back in the truck and get the hell out of here, he thought, despite feeling himself take a step forward.

My rifle, he felt his jaw tighten. *I left it beside the bed. He has access to it. He could be aiming it at me right now.*

He saw an outline of a figure behind the blinds and felt his stomach jump into his throat. He blinked and the image disappeared.

He grunted, angry with himself for falling victim to such a simple thing as his eyes playing tricks on him. Agitated, he moved toward the cottage and rounded the corner. He moved up the faded white steps of the porch and listened to the sound of the waves behind him. He used this as a reminder to take a deep breath and calm himself, as he could still feel his pulse thudding in his neck.

Satisfied that he was feeling more grounded, he pulled open the screen door and walked into the cabin. The door to Everette's room was closed, leaving the shared living room lifeless.

Art walked over to his bedroom and saw that the rifle was still leaning against the end table where he had left it. He picked up the weapon, pulled back the bolt and let the ejected round clatter to the hardwood floor.

He examined the firearm, seeing no indication that it had been tampered with or that Everette had even touched it. He felt his shoulders sag and let his mind wander.

Stop it, Art. You're just being paranoid. Out to get this guy even though he's done nothing wrong. He was probably exercising again, running around the property. Yeah, that's it. He said he had no workout clothes. He's in good shape. Good on him for jogging, especially in those shoes and jeans. Guy's feet must hurt like hell.

"How was town?" Everette's voice came from the doorway.

Art felt a chill move down his spine as he spun around to face the man. He blinked once before replying, "It was good." He lowered the weapon, leaning it against the end table in a delicate manner.

"Find everything you need?" Everette asked. His eyes clung to the firearm as Art's fingers left the weapon.

"Ya, I got everything," Art replied, but even he could hear the hesitation in his voice.

Everette made a noncommittal grunt before taking his eyes off the rifle and looking around the room. "I don't see your new cream." He paused, his voice taking on a different tone. "Can I use it?"

"Uh, ya, right here." Art opened the drawer to the end table and picked up the tube of ointment. His eyes lingered on the ammunition box that sat in the drawer beside it. He turned around and passed the cream to Everette.

"Looks like the same one you bought yesterday," Everette said as he spun the tube meekly between his hands.

How does he know what it looked like? I never showed him the kind I bought yesterday, Art thought, but kept his face calm as to not show any emotion.

"And did you end up relaxing while I was gone?" Art asked after a moment, trying to change the subject.

"I had a nap. And you're right, these beds ... not much for sleeping," Everette said, prompting Art to let out a nervous chuckle. A sliver of a smile appeared on Everette's face before he continued, "So, where's the new stuff?" He held the tube of cream in the air before tossing it on the mattress. "You said that one wasn't very good, and my back is killing me. I need the extra strength."

"Um, the store didn't have anything else," Art said, hearing himself trip over the phrasing. "Small town drugstores, you know how they are." He shrugged, feeling his palms grow sweaty as Everette continued to stand in the doorway, his grey eyes moving to the rifle once again.

"That's not what you said. I asked if you found everything, and you said yes." Everette paused, his eyes finding Art's. "So you lied."

"No..." Art began to verbally backpedal. "I found everything, as in I found everything they had." He pointed to the cream that lay on the mattress. "And that was all they had."

Everette blinked, but said nothing. He stood up straight, pivoted and returned to his room.

What a nutjob, Art thought as he kept his eyes on the empty door frame for a moment to ensure his housemate didn't return.

He turned around slowly, listening for any indication of movement before looking out the window, his eyes locked on the bend in the driveway. The rest of the world was out of sight.

Now he knows I'm onto him. I wouldn't have bought that excuse, and judging by his lack of response, neither did he. He bent down and picked up the ejected round, placing it on the table. *I'll stay another night; I need to figure this guy out. But I know one thing for certain, I ain't letting this rifle out of my sight, not even for a second.*

Someone was at the door of the cabin.

Everette heard a scraping sound as if someone was trying to force their way in. He sprung up, any sense of fear long vanished. He pulled open the door and moved into the living room.

I need to prove to that moron in the next room that I'm not crazy.

He heard the jiggling of the knob cease as he grabbed the flashlight from the mantle and switched it on. Art's snoring from the other room was deafening, but he ignored it. Moving forward, he unlocked the door and threw it open. His flashlight illuminated the screen door and the empty porch beyond.

Everette took a deep breath and pushed the screen open. The sound of heavy rain beat against his ear drums. He went outside, moving his flashlight between the two ends of the porch.

No one was there.

He moved to the left side of the deck, attempting to hear any noise over the roaring sounds of the rain to detect if anyone was moving toward him. Reaching the edge of the porch, he leaned over the wooden railing and looked down the driveway, past the vehicles and down into the black abyss that swirled just out of the flashlight's range.

He could see a figure there. He knew it.

Everette kept his light still, hoping the person would move into the beam. As he stared at the outline of the figure, his mind began to fill in the blanks. He envisioned a twisted being, drenched in seaweed with crustaceans scuttling out of long-rotten eye sockets. A gaping mouth as if shrieking in horror, but emitting no sound.

He shivered at the image his mind had concocted and let his eyes leave the figure for a moment as he attempted to compose himself.

More movement, this time in the tree line next to the vehicles.

In the short moment between when his eyes arrived at the spot and the beam of his flashlight caught up, he saw a trio of jackal-faced bipeds smiling at him with lust. Blood dripped, dripped, dripped from their teeth, falling to the untamed grass where the rainwater rushed the fluid off toward the tides of the lake.

But as the beam of light was leveled in their direction, he saw nothing. No jackals, no blood. Just the trunks of trees and piles of dead leaves that had gathered at their base. He let out a breath, a mix of relief and exasperation, before turning the flashlight back down the driveway. The outline of the figure he had seen was gone.

Everette clicked his teeth together, his mind beginning to question if what he had seen was true or simply a trick of the light. He felt a chill move over him as the nighttime air stripped him of his body heat. He lowered his torch to the spot where the driveway ceased and became the walkway up to the porch.

His eyes widened at what he saw.

A set of barefoot prints in the mud, moving down the driveway and toward the parked vehicles.

No shoes, Everette thought, his eyes studying the intricacies of the print. *That's how they are so quiet. That's why that buffoon of a beat cop can't hear them over his incessant snoring.*

Everette backed away from the railing, a sense of excitement moving through him. Now he had proof that the intruders were real, and with that proof carried the fact that Art would need to listen to him from now on.

No more second guessing everything I do, he thought, a peculiar smile tugging at his lips.

He pulled open the screen door and entered the cabin over the sounds of Art's snoring through the thin bedroom door that remained closed.

That's right, sleep. For tomorrow you are in for a rude awakening when you see those footprints and know that you were wrong about me the whole time.

He closed the door to the cabin and locked it before returning to his bedroom. He placed the flashlight on the end table beside him and looked down at his bare feet. He could see a wet leaf had affixed itself to the sole of his right foot. He wiped off his feet with a vague feeling of disgust before swinging his legs onto the bed and pulling the sheet up to his chin.

Everette slept better that night than he had in weeks.

Chapter 4

Pull Me Under, Baby

"Morning sunshine," Everette said as he leaned against the counter, a mug clasped between his palms.

"Yeah, morning," Art replied as he hobbled into the kitchen with a hunched over gait, a hand gripping his lower back.

"You sleep well last night?" Everette asked, and Art perceived it as the loaded question it was.

"Yeah, just fine. Even with the gravel that Red loads these mattresses up with." Art stood up and let out a weak groan before giving his back a twist in an attempt to stretch it. "Did you hear anyone outside in the night?"

Everette put the mug down beside him and picked at his nails for a moment before saying, "Once you're more awake, there is something I want to show you."

Art tilted his head with mild annoyance. "I'm awake now. Tell me what you want me to see."

"Telling you wouldn't do it justice. You have to see it," Everette said as he ceased cleaning his nails, his eyes meeting his housemate's.

"Fine. Let's go see it then," Art said. As Everette opened his mouth to reply, he added, "It's close, right? I don't have to drive anywhere?"

"Oh yes, it's close. Just outside," Everette replied as he stood from his leaning position. An aura of gloating clung to every word he had spoken. He moved toward the screen door and held it open, beckoning for Art to lead the way outside. "I found a set of footprints in the mud last night."

"Oh yeah? And you think these were left by the intruder?" Art asked as he passed Everette, glancing at his hands and waistband for any sign of weapons.

"I don't think; I know," Everette mumbled as he followed Art outside, the screen door shutting behind them with a loud crack. "But there is something unique about them. They're barefoot," he said, pointing toward the railing at the other end of the porch.

Art moved over to where Everette's finger indicated. He heard the footfalls behind him and could practically feel Everette breathing down his neck.

Art leaned over the railing, squinting down at the mud. He couldn't see anything that resembled the footprints Everette had described. "I don't see anything," he said finally. His gaze shifted from the uneven pebbles. "I see our shoe prints, and specifically mine from yesterday right there, but that's it."

"No, they were there. I saw them," Everette said as he moved from behind Art, his eyes frantic as he searched the same patch of ground. "I saw them. I-I—" He turned to look at Art, his eyes bulging with anger. "They were there, I know they were!"

"Yeah, you said that just a minute ago. But listen, I know from experience how moonlight can play tricks on you. Bend the shadows and twist—"

"This was no trick of shadows!" Everette's voice was raised now, his hands animated as he spoke. "I heard someone at the door. I went out to check and there they were." He stabbed the air with a finger. "Right there!"

"All right, all right. I believe you. But they aren't there now," Art replied, straightening up as his back began to ache from leaning over the railing.

"No. No they aren't." Everette's voice softened. His eyes remained pinned to Art's face. There was a moment of silence between them where only the waves could be heard before he added. "You got rid of them." He ground his teeth, adding, "You just don't want to admit I'm right. You came out here and you got rid of them."

"Woah now!" Art stood tall. "Who do you think you are, accusing me of that? Why— *How* would I even do that? And let's say I did—*which I didn't*—how would you not notice me removing these theoretical footprints? This place is not that big."

"I don't know, but every step of the way you've blocked me on this," Everette said as he began to pace. "You're part of this. You're out to get me. You're... You're trying to scare me away. You wanted this cabin to yourself so you came up with this plan—"

"You're crazy!" Art bellowed.

Everette ceased walking and said through gritted teeth. "I ... am not ... crazy!" He turned on his heels and trudged through the door, the screen slamming behind him.

Total whack job, Art thought as he followed him into the cabin. He did not trust Everette to be alone in this state.

Art entered the cottage, and to his surprise, he saw that the door to Everette's bedroom was open, his bed empty. Art's brow furrowed before he turned his attention to the kitchen and saw

Everette standing at the center, a pot of coffee in his hands. Art flinched, expecting it to be hurled in his direction, yet the pot stayed in Everette's hands as he poured himself a cup of the hot liquid.

"Coffee?" Everette asked in a neutral tone.

"What?" Art barked as he stepped to the middle of the living room.

"I asked if you wanted coffee. Yes? No?" Everette's voice was pleasant, the most pleasant Art had ever heard the man speak.

"Why? Did you poison it?" Art asked, taken aback by the complete one-hundred-and-eighty-degree change in demeanor.

Everette looked dumbfounded, his mouth opening and closing before speaking. "That's a weird joke to make."

"Weren't you just mad? I-I... What?" Art stammered as he approached the counter.

Everette brought another mug from the drying rack and began to fill it. "Oh, that? I was just screwing around."

"But the whole thing with the footsteps. You accused me of—"

"Screwing around," Everette repeated as he shook his head. He placed the pot back in the coffeemaker and said with a small grin, "Obviously you couldn't have gone out there and done all that. Like you said, I would have heard you. I'm sorry if I frightened you." He put his palm to his forehead. "Stupid temper got the better of me for a second."

"Temper?" Art asked, his brow furrowing once more. "You said you were just kidding."

"Yes," Everette replied simply, his eyes innocent.

This guy is truly certifiable, Art thought. *I need to get to town and talk to the sheriff.*

He looked down at his watch and saw it was only seven

thirty in the morning. He sighed, realizing how much time he still had with this lunatic before he could meet up with the sheriff.

Art returned his gaze to Everette and asked, "So all this is behind us then?"

"Oh, yes. Again, I apologize for frightening you."

"You didn't frighten me," Art replied as his mind spun a different tale.

I'm just worried you're going to shoot me with my own rifle.

He tugged at his beard and quickly added, "I'm glad we can be civil again."

Everette pushed the mug of coffee toward Art, passing the bag of sugar a moment later. "Oh yes, we're quite civil."

He smiled at Art, who gulped as he wrapped his fingers around the warm mug. Art watched as Everette turned on the tap and began humming "Yankee Doodle" while he rinsed off several dishes.

Art stepped out of his truck and felt the sun on the back of his neck. He walked past the sheriff's cruiser and looked down at this watch. It was half past ten. He was late. *Damn logging trucks*, he thought as he nodded at a group of retirees leaving the establishment.

As he entered the restaurant, he recalled how Everette had asked him why he was taking his rifle with him to the truck. Art had been impressed with himself by just how fast he had come up with a lie. "Ran into a guy in town yesterday," he had said. "A hunter. Wanted to take a look at it, might give me a good price on it. It's a collector's item."

Art bet that Everette wasn't much of a gun fanatic, a bet he had seemingly won judging by how Everette had nodded and gone back to reading his book.

Art thought of the rifle on its mount on the rear window of his truck. *Collector's item?* He chuckled to himself. *That thing's as common as dirt.*

The bell rang over the door and the waitress looked up from her coffee pot as she finished pouring a patron a fresh cup. "Table for one again, hun?"

Art gestured toward the sheriff who sat in the same spot as he had the day before. "Just here to see the sheriff, but I'll have a coffee."

The waitress replied but Art didn't hear her as he was already headed over toward the sheriff, who looked up at him from his paper. "Officer Billings, how are you today?" He looked out the window, past his Crown Victoria police car and to the shabby town beyond. "Glad it stopped raining?"

Art sat down and adjusted himself in the booth as he said, "Ya, it's nice. Say, any update on that record check?"

The sheriff swallowed a sip of coffee and grabbed a home fry from his plate. "Yup, and I also had a nice talk with your sergeant friend in State Grass. They still hold you in quite high esteem over there." He scratched the stubble on his chin before adding, "I hope I'm remembered that fondly when I retire."

Art smiled politely. "So, what did his record say?"

The sheriff drummed his fingers on the table for a moment as he replied, "Precisely nothing. No arrests, no crimes. Mr. Everette Davis is as clean as they come."

"Really? You found him even without the date of birth? You're sure you got the right one?"

"Nobody with that name in that age range born in May like you gave me..." He trailed off before tilting his head. "You sound disappointed. It's good news, right? Now you can rest easy."

"I don't know," Art said, running a hand through his hair. "He's acting weirder."

"How so?" the sheriff replied as he popped another home fry into his mouth.

"Talking about seeing footprints—barefoot ones, mind you —in the mud to 'prove' that there was someone outside. But I looked and didn't see a thing. Then he accused me of hiding the evidence." Art balled his hands in frustration. "Then a second later he acts like it's water under the bridge and it never happened."

"Sounds like a nutbar all right. And you say he's Red's friend as well?" The sheriff kissed his teeth. "Damn shame. Red's usually such a good judge of character."

Art shrugged as the waitress brought over his coffee. She gave him a quizzical look as if to ask if he would be ordering anything else, but once Art shook his head no, she turned and headed back toward the far side of the diner.

"I would like to think that maybe I'm just meeting him at an odd time in his life or something," Art said, pulling his mug of coffee closer. "Maybe his divorce is hitting him harder than most or ... well, I don't know, he's such an odd duck I can't see what Red sees in him. They work together so maybe at work he's normal."

The sheriff wiped his hands on a napkin beside his plate. "Well, I wish I could help, but you know as well as me, unless he actually commits a crime..." He trailed off as he reached for his wallet.

"No, let me get that for you, Sheriff," Art replied as he pulled out his own wallet. "As a thank you for looking into this for me. A token of appreciation from State Grass P.D."

The sheriff held up a hand. "No, no, I got it. I appreciate the gesture but I'm good." He placed some money on the table and stood up, adding, "Gonna head out to the marina. Someone broke in last night. Got two of my deputies looking after it but it's looking like it might be quite the case."

Art looked into the blackness of his coffee. "I miss it sometimes ... the police work, the investigating, the interviews."

The sheriff gave a curious smile before saying, "Well, feel free to stop by tomorrow for a longer chat. Sorry for cutting it short today."

Art thanked him again for the information and listened to the sound of the sheriff's boots moving toward the doorway. The bell jingled and he watched the sheriff get into his cruiser.

I don't think I'll be here tomorrow. I'm not staying another night here with Everette Davis, he thought, watching the cruiser back out of the parking lot.

As the sheriff's vehicle moved down the street, a set of grey clouds darkened the sky, threatening the little town below with another barrage of rain.

"So much for the good weather," Art mumbled to himself.

As Art drove down the country road he thought, *I'll just tell him I'm sorry to leave him in the lurch, but my son is in the hospital. A hiking accident. He'll have to finish—or I guess start —the winterizing by himself.* He gripped the steering wheel harder. *Simple as that. In twenty minutes I can be out of here. No, more like ten. Hell, I'll do it in five.*

He passed a small street on his left and knew he was a little under a mile from his turn off to the cabin. His eyes shifted to the rear-view mirror and he looked at himself, his mind focusing on Everette and his peculiar ways.

What was he doing in the woods yesterday?

Before his brain registered what was happening, he felt his foot shift from the gas to the brake, slowly compressing it. The sound of the blinker reached his ears before he even realized he had switched it on.

He pulled the truck over and shook his head. "Why do I care? I'll go tell him and leave, simple as that. Then, God willing, I never see him again," Art said to himself as he peered into the heart of the forest. The branches swayed in the breeze as a series of golden coloured leaves fell to the ground.

But I need to know why he's acting so crazy. He's just not normal.

He unbuckled his seatbelt and quickly came up with a plan. *Everette heard my truck coming yesterday; that's why he ran back to the cabin. But if I walk up, using the trees as cover, and enter the forest path behind the firewood pile, I can see what he's been up to. And if I run into him along the way I'll just say my truck broke down or something.*

As the thought left his mind, he shuddered at what the bill would be to have his vehicle towed all the way back to town for his cover not to be blown.

Art turned off the engine and exited the truck, feeling the refreshing air on his face as he shut the door and locked his truck. He began his walk down the shoulder of the road, his footing uneven as the pebbles gave way under his shoes.

After several minutes he shrugged to himself, thinking, *And if I don't find anything, then I don't find anything. But at least I'll know. I guess I'll have to take what he said about exercising as the truth and chalk it up to a crazy man doing crazy things.*

He reached the turn off for the cabin and looked down the winding driveway. All was quiet save for a gust of sea wind that moved toward him. He licked his lips, pushing down the peculiar feeling that he was doing something illegal.

He walked down the driveway until he could just see the cabin through the twisted branches. Then he left the road and headed into the tree line in the direction where the path would be. He felt twigs snap off his chest and kept a raised hand in front of his head to stop from being poked in the face. All the while he kept an eye on the cabin and the property perimeter.

No Everette in sight.

Maybe he's reading on the porch. Art cringed upon snapping an exceptionally loud twig underfoot. He waited a moment before continuing to walk. *He kept saying he wished the weather was nicer so he could sit outside and watch the water.*

With no small effort, Art eventually reached the forest path. He turned his head to look in both directions. He was still alone. He headed to his right, following the path deeper into the woods.

He walked for several minutes until he came to a spot where the foliage created a darkened space. He saw shoe prints, and there was no doubt they belonged to Everette. They headed forward for a while before changing direction and leading off the forest path. Art could also see another pair of tracks returning to the path beside the originals, except these ones headed back toward the cabin.

What have you been doing out here?

Art looked over his shoulder once more before following the prints off the beaten path. He pushed through bushes and could see further evidence that Everette had been there by the snapped branches and crushed leaves. He walked on until he came to it.

A mound of dirt and mud.

Art's pulse quickened. The dirt was piled a few inches higher than the ground. Everette had tried unsuccessfully to flatten it out but had seemingly given up. The hole was rectangular, and Art estimated it to be a little longer than five feet.

What the hell could he have buried?

He stared at the mound for a long time, his mind replaying every interaction with Everette in the days prior. He thought back to his policing days, his brain working toward the most likely scenario given the information at hand.

Whatever it is, it's big. But what could he want buried so bad that he waited until he came all the way up here?

The sudden realization struck him harder than the bullet to his shoulder had.

His wife.

Art clutched his chest in an attempt to control his breathing. He looked around, now aware of how painfully alone and completely vulnerable he was. No one was around to help him if Everette discovered him skulking in a place he shouldn't be.

He listened to the sounds of a slight breeze pushing past the trees, but heard no sign that Everette was nearby. He turned back to face what he now realized was a grave, his mind spinning.

It all makes sense. The divorce, his weird looks whenever I brought her up, Red not knowing they had split up. He bent down and began to claw at the dirt, pulling up thick fistfuls of mud. *He killed her last week when he called in sick and waited to come out here to bury her. To hide it. But how did no one notice she'd gone missing?*

He pulled up another clump of dirt before stopping. *If he buried her six feet down I'll be here for hours. I have to tell the sheriff.* He stood up and could see the evidence of his presence was all over the grave. *If Everette comes back here when I'm gone, he'll know someone found her. He'll run, or move the body or—*

Art bent down again, a shooting pain racing down his back as he did so. He did his best to flatten out the pile of mud.

While it was not identical to how it had been, it was close enough that Everette likely wouldn't notice.

Art stood, his head spinning with an intense combination of adrenaline and fear.

I have to tell the sheriff.

He bounded back the way he had come, his body aching at the sudden jolt of exercise. He looked down and realized he was leaving footprints in the path, just as Everette had. He shook his head and continued as he could think of no way to cover them up.

I just have to hope he doesn't come back here.

———

Art flew up to the sheriff's office at the north end of town, having just broken every speed law in the state. He hopped out of the truck and ran into the modest station.

"I need to see the sheriff," he wheezed to the receptionist who sat behind a thin pane of glass.

A deputy located at the back of the office looked up from his file, a concerned expression on his face. As he stood, he said, "The sheriff's out right now, can I help you?"

The deputy looked no older than twenty-five, and his uniform radiated with a newly issued glow. Art's eyes focused on the shining badge that gleamed brightly on his chest as he asked, "Where's the sheriff?" A bead of sweat raced down his temple.

The deputy held up his hands. "Woah, before we get him involved maybe I can—"

"Look, this might involve murder. I need to talk to him now."

The deputy took a step back, placing his hands on his belt like he wasn't sure what to do with them. "A murder? Who's?"

"Is he still at the marina?" Art replied, ignoring the deputy's oddly phrased question.

The deputy looked to the receptionist and gulped. "Uh, no. He's at the mayor's office. I can call him—"

"Yes, call him and give me the phone. I need to talk to him."

The deputy grabbed the phone from the counter and dialed the numbers. After a few moments he spoke again, "Hey there, Rosey. It's Deputy Baker calling. Yes, that's right. Do you mind getting him? Okay, I'll wait right here." He put his hand over the receiver as he informed Art, "She's gonna grab him." He gave Art a once over before adding, "What's your name?"

"Art Billings. I've met him before; he knows who I am."

The deputy returned the phone to his ear before saying, "Hey there, Sheriff; it's Reid. Listen, I got a fella here who wants to talk to you, a Mr. Art Billings. Yup. Uh... Yeah, I told him, but he said it's about murder and—"

"Give me the phone," Art said, prompting Deputy Baker to push it through the slit under the glass. Art grabbed the phone from the deputy's outstretched hand and said, "I found a body."

"You did?" The sheriff gasped on the other end of the line. "Who's?"

"I think it's his wife. I mean, I haven't actually seen it yet. It's buried. But I—"

"So you found a body, or you didn't?"

"I found a mound of dirt in the woods behind the cottage, Everette's shoe prints going to and from it. It's off the beaten path. He's buried something back there." There was a long delay and then, "You still there, Sheriff?"

"Ya, I'm here. But..." There was a sigh into the receiver. "All right, I'll come back to the station and we'll go talk to Mr. Everette Davis. But realistically there could be anything back there, maybe a wild animal. I mean, to accuse a man of murder just because you don't like him?"

"Sheriff, it's not that. It's—"

"I'm coming out there, but..." He paused again, noticeably longer this time before continuing. "If you didn't have such good reviews from your sergeant, I would be handling this quite differently."

"Trust me, Sheriff. I can prove it."

Chapter 5

Nebulous Seas

Art led the two police cruisers up the driveway and parked behind Everette's car. He got out of the truck and watched as the sheriff exited the vehicle directly behind him. The two deputies—Deputy Baker and another that Art hadn't spoken with yet—stepped out of the rear cruiser.

Art looked toward the windows of the cabin and saw the blinds in Everette's room flutter. "Got you now, you son of a bitch," he said aloud to himself.

He looked to his rifle that was placed on its mount and contemplated grabbing it, but realized the officers would tell him to leave it behind for everyone's safety. Art closed the door to his vehicle and made eye contact with the sheriff, who held a face of uncertainty as he met Art's gaze.

The four men walked along the side of the cabin, the sheriff and deputies having now taken the lead. Art could see that Deputy Baker was trembling slightly, but he quickly adjusted his hat to mask it. The other deputy carried himself with more confidence, and his uniform was noticeably more worn.

The sheriff knocked on the door which prompted Art to say, "You can go in, Sheriff. You have permission."

"Let me handle this, okay?" the sheriff said over his shoulder prior to Everette opening the door. The creak of the hinges brought his attention forward. "Afternoon, sir," the sheriff straightened up, his voice becoming more authoritative. "Do you mind if we come in and ask you a few questions?"

"What's this about?" Everette snapped. His fingers dug into the side of the door as he gripped it white knuckled.

"The disappearance of your wife."

Everette cocked his head and released the door. "Well, investigation over, because she's not missing."

Because you killed her and buried her out back. You know exactly where she is, Art thought as he watched the sheriff with eager anticipation.

"Do you mind if we come in and talk about it?" the sheriff replied, undeterred.

Everette moved away from the door, a look of annoyance on his face. "I guess. Come in then."

"Good. It's more of a courtesy. I already called Red and he said we could enter the home, but thank you for agreeing." All four men entered. Art stayed near the door, and the sheriff studied Everette with a peculiar eye.

"Like I said, she's not missing," Everette said as he sat in a chair beside the fireplace. "I don't know what there is left to talk about."

"Can you prove she's not missing?" the sheriff asked.

"Well what kind of question is that? Who can prove anything?"

Something a guilty person would say, Art thought as he glared at Everette, who shifted his weight in his chair.

"Where is she now then?" the sheriff asked as he began to look around the living room, his eyes pausing on Everette's room before turning his attention to the man sitting in front of him.

"How the hell should I know? She is my *ex*-wife. She's a free woman, as she always liked to point out." Venom spewed from Everette's lips. "Like I said, I don't know where she would be!" He stabbed the air with a finger, uttering each syllable of the last mouthful of words.

Art could see in his peripheral that Deputy Baker was eying the sheriff for any sign of an order. His hand resting on his handcuff pouch.

"If you were to guess where she is, maybe that would help us," the sheriff said after a moment.

"Who's buried in the back?" Art blurted out as he looked at Everette's boney face. He could not bear to wait for this run around to cease.

Everette shot him a glance before addressing the sheriff in a calm voice. "No one is buried in the back. And what, are you following me or something? Stalking me? Isn't that a crime, Sheriff?" His gaze zoomed in on Art. "Watching my every little move? Is that what you've been doing?"

"Look, Mr. Davis, Art here has found a peculiar spot behind the house. Now, I can go back there and start digging, but I thought I would let you explain yourself."

"You honestly think I murdered my wife?" Everette said, ignoring the sheriff, his grey eyes still fixated on Art.

The sheriff snapped his fingers in front of Everette's face. "Mr. Davis, I'm over here." He waited until Everette made eye contact before continuing, "So, should I go out back and start digging?"

"Fine, you want me to prove I'm not lying and didn't murder Tammy? Fine. Fine!" He stood up and Deputy Baker took a step forward, his hand shifting to the club on his belt.

The sheriff didn't move a muscle. "I'll call her, how about that?" He moved to the phone and began to dial.

I'm sure it will go to the answering machine, and he'll shrug and say, "I guess she's not home. Must be out shacking up with every Tom, Dick and Harry." Or—

"Tammy! Hi, yeah, don't hang up; it's serious. Look... Look, wait! The police are here ... at the cottage. Yeah, they want to talk to you." Everette lowered the receiver before passing it to the sheriff. "Good luck," he said before retreating to his seat.

The sheriff looked at the phone in his hand for a moment before directing a dirty look toward Art. He raised the receiver to his ear. "Hello, Mrs. Davis? This is Sheriff Hainsworth, I was — Yes, I know you're divorced. Oh, my apologies, it's Miss Abbot now. Right... So you are currently where, then? Oh, okay. And you are well and all that?"

Sheriff Hainsworth looked to Everette for a moment before saying, "Is there anything you would like to say about your ex-husband that pertains to this, um, investigation." He sounded as if he was struggling to come up with things to say. "Yes, well I will not be repeating that. All right, sorry to bother you Mrs. Dav— Abbot. Thank you for your time."

The sheriff hung up the phone and Everette spoke first. "Piece of work, or am I wrong?" He sat with his arms crossed, a self-satisfied expression on his face.

The sheriff ignored the comment, instead glaring at Art for several moments. He slowly turned to face Everette and said, "I'm sorry to waste your time, sir."

"That could have been anyone," Art stammered. "A girl-friend of his, or his sister. There is no proof that was his wife—"

The sheriff shook his head, prompting Art to cease speaking. "Oh, that was his ex-wife. I've never heard a woman use such profanities before. There is no doubt in my mind that she is alive and well."

"I don't know if she's *well*," Everette muttered. His expression looked as if he was rather bored of the whole thing.

"Come on, gentlemen. Let's go," Sheriff Hainsworth said, looking between his two deputies.

"No, there's more! The body in the back!" Art nearly screamed the words.

The sheriff sighed and the two deputies turned to look at Art. The sheriff directed his question to Everette. "So, Mr. Davis, anything to say about that?"

Everette bit his lip. "Look, I proved to you my ex-wife is alive. What more do I have to do? Am I being detained? Do I have to answer your questions?"

"No, Mr. Davis, you aren't being detained and you don't have to answer questions. But like I said, Red already gave me permission to move about the property as I see fit. So either you tell me what's back there or I start digging."

Everette's eyes moved between Art and the sheriff several times before saying, "All right, I hit a deer. About an hour from here. A baby deer. It ran right in front of me. I couldn't leave it there on the side of the road, broken little legs. I had to bury it."

Tears began to form in his eyes as he continued, "My mother always said people should be more decent and bury innocent animals when they die, not just leave them to rot in the sun. I guess I should have called a park ranger or you, but I didn't know. I mean, I know to hunt deer you need a license, and I don't have one, so I guess that's a crime—but I wasn't hunting, I was driving. I guess that's it." He looked to the sheriff, his hands raised. "So you're going to arrest me for moving a dead animal?" His face depicted a side that Art had not seen before. He looked genuinely grief stricken.

"No." The sheriff shook his head, his face radiating annoyance. "I'm not arresting you for hitting a deer."

"Sheriff, don't listen to him; he's lying. There's no damage to his car—"

"Yes there is." Everette balled his hands into fists. "I can show you. Probably more than two hundred dollars' worth. I don't know, I'm not a mechanic. All I know is I can't afford it, not when Tammy is going to take me for everything I've got!"

"Let's go look at it," the sheriff said, his eyes passing over the occupants of the room.

"Fine. Are we done here after that? Because I was about to make something to eat," Everette said as he rose to his feet.

"Let's look at the damage first," the sheriff said, but his voice had lost its gusto.

They all walked outside, Everette in the lead. The older deputy pulled out a cigarette and lit it. Clearly, he had already deemed Everette innocent and didn't consider him a threat. Deputy Baker looked noticeably less stressed as well.

"There's the damage," Everette said, and gestured to the front bumper.

The sheriff bent down and pushed on the bumper with his palm, seeing that it hung a little lower on the passenger side, along with a small dent. "Scratches on the hood too when it toppled over onto my car. From its paws or whatever," Everette said, a note of annoyance hanging in his tone.

"Hooves," Sheriff Hainsworth said, running his fingers over several shallow streaks of silver that stopped a quarter of the way up the hood.

"Not much damage for hitting a deer," Art jeered.

"A baby deer, separated from its mama," Everette said as his eyes gravitated to his shoes. "I feel terrible about the whole thing, really."

The sheriff chewed his lip before saying, "Sorry about all this, Mr. Davis." He motioned to his deputies, and they began to head back to their cruisers.

"But, Sheriff," Art called as he jogged after them, "the grave site? Shouldn't you dig down and—"

Sheriff Hainsworth turned. "I am not wasting any more time on this. You want to go digging, feel free. But this here has been a big waste of time." His nostrils flared. "You have some vendetta against this guy and I just don't get it. You've been wrong at every turn. The criminal record check, the wife already being dead, the lack of damage to his car.

"Frankly you should consider yourself lucky I don't bring you in for falsifying a police report. If I were you, I would leave now, because if I was that guy back there, I would seriously consider thrashing you, which I think would be mighty justified, given everything you've put him through. What do you think, Deputy Edwards?" The sheriff looked over his shoulder at the more seasoned of the two junior officers.

"I wouldn't stop him," Deputy Edwards said between puffs of his cigarette, his voice a gravelly mess.

"Right. So good day, Mr. Billings. I would say it's been a pleasure but..." He shook his head and walked away.

Art watched the police officers enter their respective cruisers and begin to back up before turning their vehicles around on the grass. Everette stood beside his car, a sullen expression on his face.

Art pushed past him, saying nothing.

He headed into the cabin, grabbed his things and was inside his truck within ninety seconds.

The truck tires spun briefly in the mud as Art slammed it into reverse. He gripped the steering wheel tight as he backed onto the grass just as the cruisers had and turned the truck around. He looked in the rear-view mirror and saw Everette giving a half-hearted wave.

The run-down truck thundered around the bend of the driveway and onto the highway beyond.

Everette cut the sandwich he had made diagonally and watched the mustard dribble down both sides of the incision. He licked his lips as he removed the pint of ice-cream from the freezer and filled a bowl with an unhealthy portion.

He was in fine spirits, and the events of the day had caused him to work up quite an appetite. He sat on the couch, eating his meal in silence, feeling satisfied and warm as he finished off the last sips of coffee.

Everette washed the dishes and looked to the wall-mounted clock next to the fridge. It had been exactly one hour since his housemate had left with his tail between his legs. He dried his hands on a tea towel and grabbed his keys from the counter before heading outside. *It's been enough time to see if that ape will show his face around here.*

Everette smiled to himself, knowing full well that Art had not left anything behind as he had checked the house thoroughly to ensure there would be no reason for him to return.

He headed toward his car at a lackadaisical pace, hardly aware he was walking as he moved about in a trance.

Upon arriving at his sedan, he ran his hand over the hood, his fingers meeting the scratches. *Thank God I hit that deer,* he thought as he moved to the rear of the vehicle and opened the trunk.

Inside was a jumble of construction plastic and tarps laying underneath a mud-encrusted shovel. Everette looked at the dried blood that slicked the plastic before his fingers snatched a blue shawl that was tucked toward the back.

He held the garment tight as he sealed the trunk, his eyes wandering in the direction of where she was buried as he muttered, "That will teach her to tell Tammy about us."

Everette walked away from his car and headed to the

waterfront, shawl in hand. He moved toward the chair and chilled beer he had set up several minutes' prior.

"Now I can relax," he said as he sat down and held the garment to his nose.

He could still smell her perfume.

Chapter 6

Diver Down

Art sat in his vehicle, his gaze fixed to the front entrance of the hardware store where people came and went with leisure. He had driven over an hour away from the cottage in the direction of home and stopped in the first town that contained more than two gas stations and a bar.

He heard a family chatting as they entered their station wagon beside him. Once they left, he looked at himself in the rear-view mirror and said, "I have to know."

He exited his truck and walked through the sliding entrance doors, moving toward the back of the store where a large *Gardening* sign hung from the metal joists of the dusty ceiling. He patrolled an aisle of various trimming tools, stopping at the rack of shovels.

As his fingers wrapped around the wooden shaft of the nearest one, he thought, *I know he did it. I just know it, and if that makes me the crazy one then...*

He paused, his arm still outstretched as the thought changed direction. *But the sheriff's right, I have no proof. I was wrong about the wife, wrong about him having a record, wrong about the lack of damage to his car.*

He felt his fingers release from the item. *What am I doing here? Why can't I just admit that I'm wrong on this, wrong about him? Admit that I've lost my intuition? Six years sitting around in an unwanted retirement, fixing small engines has sapped me of my instinct.*

Art stepped back from the shovel, eyeing it with contempt. After a moment he began to walk away, his pulse pounding in his ears. Just as he reached the end of the aisle another thought occurred to him, this one clearer than all the others:

But who the hell buries a deer after hitting it, and an hour away from where you're heading? And for a baby deer, no one digs a hole that big.

Art pivoted, seized the shovel and marched toward the cash register. *If I'm wrong, that's the end of it and I'll rebury the goddamn deer. But if I'm right...*

His mind turned to the rifle mounted on the back window of his truck.

———

The sun had already set by the time Art brought his truck to a halt a half mile from the cottage driveway. He shut off the engine and opened the door with deliberate care to avoid the familiar creaking of the old vehicle. He flexed his back and grabbed the rifle from its mount, then opened the box of bullets he kept under the seat and loaded the weapon. He then grabbed five additional rounds and put them in the pocket of his jeans.

He was not taking any chances.

Art closed the door and walked to the bed of the truck. He felt the chill of the night about him as he removed the newly purchased shovel, opened a dinged-up toolbox and pulled out a flashlight. He looked down the road in the direction he had come. Now with the absence of headlights, the boulevard looked barren and abandoned.

Art felt completely alone.

He gulped and walked down the road toward the cabin where Everette Davis had turned in for the night. He was likely sound asleep, but that wouldn't last for much longer.

Everette awoke to the sound of the screen door banging. He opened his eyes and saw that his bedroom door was open, allowing him to see that the main entrance to the cabin was as well. The screen door repeatedly blew open and shut in the breeze.

"Everette," the voice whispered from over top of him.

He jerked up, but became twisted in the sheets, falling out of bed. His eyes darted around the dark room, finally resting upwards as he could see what looked like matted hair hanging down from the black void above.

The outline took form then, and she was there, clinging to the ceiling. Her neck was twisted and broken, her hollow eyes watching him.

"Everette," she called again.

He flipped onto his front and crawled out into the living room, grabbing the flashlight from the fireplace in one fluid motion as he stood. He pointed it at the ceiling. The beam illuminated nothing but faded stucco.

"You killed me, Everette." The voice came from behind and he felt his heart jump out of his chest. He stifled a scream and spun around.

No one was there.

"It was your fault," he said, looking every which way around the living room. "You told her! What did you want me to do? You ruined it all with your big stupid mouth!" He spoke with a crazed twinge in his eyes, while spit coated the brick-work of the fireplace. "You could never shut the fuck up, could you?"

There were footsteps outside on the gravel path. Slow. Monotonous.

"What choice did I have?" His voice had changed to a quiver.

The footsteps grew nearer. He ran to the open door and threw it shut, locking it with trembling hands. The footsteps continued up the wooden steps.

"What do you want?" Everette pleaded, the beam of light shaking against the door, his back to the wall.

"Turn yourself in, Everette," the voice called from the kitchen.

He jerked the light toward the source of the command, but as the light pierced the blackness, the woman's silhouette disappeared. He lunged to the counter and grabbed his car keys.

"I can't do that. I won't! Y-you bitch!" His light was turning every which way now.

The door unlocked and swung open.

"Turn yourself in, Everette," the voice echoed, reverberating around his skull.

"I can't. I—" Everette began to say, but ceased as the figure moved to his right, mere inches away. The eyes were black, blood running down outstretched arms.

The flashlight died then.

Everette screamed and threw the torch in the direction of the figure. He ran toward the front door, heading into the night.

I have to move the body, he thought. *I have to move it.*

He felt pain in his feet as he ran down the gravel path before the terrain switched to the mud of the driveway.

I'll burn it. Yeah, that's it! And bury the ashes! She can't haunt me without a body. That's right; I'll fry her up good.

Everette raced toward the rear of his car, threw open the trunk and grabbed the shovel. "Burn it! Burn it! Burn it!" he repeated to himself like a mantra as he ran off toward the treeline.

———

Art heard something in the distance and ceased his shoveling. He looked past the pile of dirt he had created and studied the woods. His flashlight sat on the ground and was facing away from the cabin to avoid being seen. He listened for several seconds but heard nothing and resumed his digging.

Almost there, he thought as he swung another load of dirt over his shoulder. He wiped the sweat from his face and dug again, his shovel penetrating the loose earth once more, twice, three times—

There was a thud.

Art used his shovel to probe at the object. It felt like a rock. A big one.

It's too hard to be a body. He moved the shovel over a few inches and tried again, but was met with the same result. *He couldn't have brought cinderblocks with him, could he?*

He dug out some of the loose dirt and widened the hole as sweat dripped into his eyes. He picked up his flashlight and shone it into the space, but still could not see what was impeding his progress.

Art got down to his knees and brushed the dirt away, repositioning the flashlight as he did so. *What is that?* He thought before pushing the last of the muck away before recognizing the hard-sided object for what it was.

A suitcase.

He returned the flashlight to the side of the hole and with great effort, pulled the suitcase from its resting place. He looked at the latches and after seeing they had no locks on them, he snapped them open.

Inside was an assortment of women's clothes.

"I was right," he said aloud in a harsh whisper.

The sudden sound of his own voice caused a chill to move up his spine. He pushed the suitcase off to the side of the hole and shone the light down into the gap where the luggage had been.

A battered face stared up at him from behind a veil of long, greasy hair, matted with mud.

He had seen dead bodies before, but it never became easier for him. Art felt his heart sink, his mind trying to process all the emotions that overcame him in that moment. He cursed himself that he was right, that Everette had not only been behind it, but that this woman was no longer alive to see her killer brought to justice.

He rubbed a hand across his face and tried to slow his breathing. But over the sound of his racing heart, he heard something, and as he listened further, he recognized the sounds for the heavy footfalls they were. Someone was coming down the forest path and approaching at a reckless pace.

Shit, shit, shit, Art thought, and switched off his light.

He picked up his shovel and pulled himself out of the hole. He grabbed his rifle from the ground and dove into the bushes, leaving the lifeless eyes of the young woman to gaze up at the sliver of the moon through the thin forest canopy.

Everette moved down the path, his feet aching under him.

Quick and easy, I dig the bitch up and then put her in the fire pit. Gasoline, a whole can of it is what I need. I'll use the axe in the shed to split her up. Two fires, so it's quicker.

While he lacked a flashlight, he had made this walk multiple times. He knew exactly where the turn off to the grave was. *Right at the tree with the misshapen trunk,* he thought, a sense of pride clinging to his thoughts at his foresight for picking such an easily identifiable landmark.

He felt a sense of excitement rise up from his stomach as he recognized the tree ahead by the light of the moon. *Bingo was his name-o.* A smile flicked upon his face over the sounds of his panting.

Everette turned off the path and stepped into the bush. His smile was short lived as the sensation of searing pain from the twigs and thistles burrowing into his feet became clear.

Half an hour tops, he thought as he moved toward Gloria's grave. *Maybe an hour because I have to drag her down to the pit. Then another hour for it to burn. More gasoline will speed that...*

His eyes took a moment to adjust to what he was seeing. Everette blinked several times as his brain fired back a single word to his consciousness:

Clothes?

He bent down and picked up a piece of fabric, his eyes then registering the open suitcase underneath the blouse.

No. No...

He stepped forward, his gaze shifting down into the grave.

His eyes never met the body as all went blank, his ears registering a hard metallic thump.

Art dragged Everette's sagging body from the bushes and onto the forest path. He let him down and watched his chest rise and fall. "I should have shot you," he said to the unconscious Everette. "Then I wouldn't have to drag you. My back would have thanked me."

He tried to collect his breath but let out a gasp as the searing pain from his shoulder returned for another assault. He lifted Everette by the shoulders and began to drag him again, swearing as he did so.

After several paces he felt Everette begin to stir in his arms. He dropped him to the dirt, unslung his weapon from his back and whacked the degenerate in the head with the wooden stock. Everette's already broken nose disintegrated from the blow and his body went limp again.

"Honestly, if I killed you, I would be doing the world a favor."

Art picked up Everette once again and dragged him until he reached the mouth of the forest path. He looked over his shoulder and saw the wall of rotting firewood on his right side. The sounds of shifting waters emanated from his left. He looked behind him. The car and the cabin sat in the distance.

They were still quite far away.

"Christ, my back," Art said through gritted teeth as he let Everette down, caring little that his head thumped off the ground.

The thought of pulling Everette all the way to the cabin made his already screaming shoulder cry out in pain. He rubbed it and looked toward the lake. Several dozen meters away was the shed. While it was rusty and downtrodden, a small flicker of hope entered his mind at the sight of it.

Maybe there's something to bind him with. Long enough for the sheriff to come out and—

Everette let out a muffled groan.

Art looked down at the sorry excuse for a human and unslung his rifle again. "Shut up!" he said before he brought the weapon down with all his might. He heard a wet crunch beneath him and knew he had dislodged several teeth.

As Everette's body went limp again, Art worried for a moment whether he had hit him too hard this time. But as his eyes moved to the torso area, he saw Everette's chest rise and fall with short, shallow breaths.

I won't lose any sleep if he dies, Art thought before picking up Everette and dragging him toward the shed.

———

Sheriff James Hainsworth stirred in bed as the phone on the nightstand rang out.

"What?" he asked, rubbing the sleep from his eyes with a free hand as the other clutched the receiver. "I mean, hello?"

He pushed his head toward his shoulder, so the phone was stationary. His wife grunted beside him and rolled over, falling back to sleep immediately.

"Sorry to bother you, Sheriff." The voice of Deputy Baker came through the speaker and Hainsworth could hear how anxious he sounded. "That Art Billings guy called."

"What does he want?" Hainsworth asked, fully awake now.

"He said he found a body. Says he went back to Red Jennings' property and dug her up. Says he immobilized that Everette guy; charged at him."

The sheriff began to get out of bed. "What else did he say?"

"He says he has him tied up and is holding him until we get there."

"I'm coming. Get in the cruiser." He paused and stopped moving to avoid pulling the phone off the table. "Is Edwards still on traffic duty? Radio him, have him meet you somewhere.

Get to Red's and call Forrest, tell him to get to the station to run it while we are out dealing with this. I'll meet you there."

"Where? At the station or—"

"At Red's property. Get moving and radio Edwards, I want you both en route immediately."

He hung up the phone and moved over to his closet, grabbing a pair of uniform pants and a fresh shirt.

He was right. I can't believe it, Hainsworth thought as he tucked in his shirt and grabbed his duty belt.

Art sat in a chair next to the fireplace, his rifle across his lap. Everette leaned back on the couch across from him. His hands and feet were tied with copious layers of duct tape. Art had thought about taping his mouth shut but was concerned he would suffocate on his own blood.

"Who was she, Everette?" Art asked as the bleeding man glared at him, an inhuman twinkle in his eyes.

Everette let out a long cough before resuming his silence. His gaze moved to the barrel of the gun.

Art heard the sounds of approaching vehicles but kept his eyes locked on his prisoner. A few moments passed and he saw the reflection of headlights appear in the kitchen window. The sounds of engines grew louder before he heard the thump of doors closing.

Bootsteps on the gravel path prompted Everette to turn his attention to the open door. He coughed again. Sheriff Hainsworth and two deputies walked up the steps, hands on their holsters.

"I'm here, Sheriff," Art called out and the officers opened the screen door and entered.

"Sheriff," Everette wheezed. "Thank God. Look what he

did!" His words were slurred, tripping over several syllables due to his lack of teeth. "I'm in so much pain."

Hainsworth ignored him, but Deputy Baker looked concerned. The sheriff took on a calm tone as he knelt beside Art. "Let's put that gun down now. No need for it."

Art complied and lowered the rifle to the floor, but kept his eyes on Everette, who coughed again before saying, "Sheriff, he has it out for me. It's like you—"

The sheriff stood tall, his attention now focused squarely on Everette. "I am detaining you on suspicion of murder. You have the right to remain silent..."

He continued with the Miranda rights, but Everette whined and rolled his head around, trying to drown out the sheriff.

"Do you have your own lawyer?" Hainsworth asked as he gestured to the second deputy to move toward him.

Everette spat toward the sheriff. The wad of clotted blood travelled less than a foot in the pitiful attempt.

Hainsworth looked at the blood on the carpet before adding, "I'll take that as you can't afford one. One will be appointed to you. Do you understand what I've said?"

Everette stared at him, a catlike smile scuttling across his face revealing several missing teeth and more clotted blood.

"Deputy Baker," the sheriff said over his shoulder, "notate the time and mark that the subject refused to answer." He let out an agitated breath before saying, "Do you wish to call a lawyer?"

"Yes," Everette croaked, the smile still glued to his face.

"Baker, notate that," the sheriff replied, looking over his shoulder before facing Everette again. "We will call one when it is safe to do so." He looked around the room. "But not here. Can't have you tampering with anything at a crime scene. Maybe the hospital will be best."

"I don't want a doctor."

"You get one anyway." The sheriff looked toward Art. "You want to show me the body?"

Art got to his feet and Hainsworth gestured to his counterparts. "Baker, Edwards, stay here. Make sure Mr. Davis doesn't go anywhere and get some handcuffs on him."

"He's not going anywhere," Deputy Edwards said, his hands glued to his holster.

Art led the sheriff outside, around the corner and past the shed where the open door swung in the breeze. As they walked down the forest path, Hainsworth spoke first, "What brought you back here? Did you even leave?"

Art kept his flashlight pointed forward; his eyes focused on the beam. "I left, but I had to know if my intuition was really that far gone. I wish I had been wrong; I really do."

They turned off the path and arrived at the gravesite. Hainsworth's eyes lingered on the open suitcase before directing his attention to the body at the bottom of the hole. "Made it look like she was skipping town," he said after a sigh. "I'll call the guys from the city, have them down here by first light. In the meantime, let's get you and that animal to the hospital."

"I don't need the hospital, I'm fine. I'll stay and watch over the body."

"Well, that's good of you, but I can't have a civilian doing that. Muddies the case and continuity of evidence," Hainsworth replied, prompting Art to nod in understanding. "I'll have Edwards set up here, get the pictures and the tape out..." He trailed off. "Damn, the camera's at the station." He shook his head. "No matter, one thing at a time."

"Getting Everette into the cruiser?" Art asked, his eyes still on the woman's cold face, his voice distant. "That's what's next?"

"Getting Everette into the cruiser," the sheriff repeated before letting out a long breath. His eyes followed the beam of Art's flashlight. "Crying shame."

Everette Davis sat in a cell at the Heartford Meadow Sheriff's Station. Hainsworth stood over him saying, "You'll be taken before a judge later this morning."

Everette ignored him and rubbed his bruised wrists from how tight the handcuffs had been. The sheriff shook his head before closing the cell door behind him. It was clear he was keeping his thoughts to himself.

The cell occupant stared dead ahead, reflecting on his short phone conversation with the lawyer while at the hospital. *I don't even know why I wanted to talk to that idiot. He said the same two things over and over. "Don't say anything; don't do anything." I could have been a lawyer if that's all I had to do. Useless.*

Everette spat out one of the cotton pads that had been placed in his mouth to soak up the blood. He recalled how the sheriff had put up a fuss about the doctor leaving them in his mouth, but the doctor had said it was mandatory or he could suffocate in the night.

Recalling the doctor, Everette thought, *That asshole put that tube down my nose. He wasn't happy when I tore it out.* Everette thought of the doctor's face and the disgusted visage he had worn. He lay down on the lumpy mattress and rubbed his face on the pillow. *They will have to clean up my mess. My bloody mess,* he thought, and closed his eyes.

He heard the light click above him and through his closed eyelids could tell the cell had gone dark. *Finally, some peace and quiet.*

He went to roll over when he heard the voice.

"Everette."

His eyes snapped open. Gloria's silhouette stood at the far end of the cell. Her long hair hung down over her blue shirt. Clumps of mud fell off her as she stepped forward, arms outstretched, feet bare.

"You should have burned me, Everette," she said as her face twisted into a smile. "You should have burned me."

Everette screamed his throat raw, but by the time the deputies arrived, the man had lost his mind.

Sheriff Hainsworth pushed a mug of coffee to his mouth after having just returned from the hospital for the second time that morning. Everette was currently in the care of the mental health wing. Deputy Forrest had been tasked with guard duty as he had to dismiss Edwards and Baker, who had been approaching a twenty-two-hour shift. He rubbed his face in an attempt to think, as it was mid-morning and he was running on less than two hours of sleep.

He grabbed the VHS tape that contained the security footage he was curious about and pushed it into the player. He pressed play and saw four different camera feeds had been recorded. The one in the bottom right of the TV captured his attention as it displayed the cell where Everette had been when he experienced his episode.

Hainsworth fast-forwarded the tape, watched as the cell suddenly became lively and saw himself remove the handcuffs from Everette, who promptly threw himself on the bed in the corner.

Hainsworth stopped fast forwarding and let the tape play. He watched as he spoke to Everette for a moment, but due to there being no sound, he couldn't hear his words. He saw himself exit the cell and close the door behind him. He squinted at the images, wondering what it was that had turned Everette from a silent psychopath into a screaming lunatic inside of five minutes.

Everette rolled onto his side just before the lights to the cell went out.

Hainsworth blinked. *How did that happen?*

He lifted his mug from the desk and took a sip. He waited and could see movement in the dark from the little bit of light emanating from under the cell door, but it wasn't enough to make out what was going on. Only that Everette sat up right and was squirming.

This must be when he started yelling, he realized, his eyes searching the darkness for an answer as to why.

The light snapped on and the cell door opened as Deputy Baker rushed in, followed immediately by Edwards. In that fraction of a second between the lights coming on and the cell door being opened, Hainsworth thought he saw something that had not been there before.

He screwed up his face as he rewound the tape to when the lights had switched off. He raised his coffee to his mouth and hit pause just as the lights snapped on.

His mug clattered to the floor, shattering into a dozen pieces.

The image on the TV displayed a woman standing in the cell. Her grey hands were wrapped around Everette's throat.

Chapter 7

Coming Up For Air

Art Billings sat in the usual booth in Heartford Meadow's cozy diner. He poured a spoonful of sugar into his coffee and listened to the tinkling of metal against porcelain. He looked to his left and admired the rain as it beaded down the glass in its race to return to the earth.

The bell over the door rang out, prompting him to turn his attention to the entrance. Sheriff Hainsworth entered, pulling his hat from his head and brushing off the excess rainwater that had collected on it. He exchanged pleasantries with one of the cooks that was bussing tables before moving in Art's direction. While Hainsworth's face had a soft smile upon it, the bags under his eyes told a different story.

Art began to stand in an effort to greet him, but Hainsworth indicated it was not necessary and took a seat across from him. As they shook hands the officer said, "I appreciate you sticking around these last few days. How's the hotel been treating you?"

"It's nice. Good showers and that view can't be beat," Art replied as he returned to stirring his coffee.

"And has Kim been giving you the VIP rate I mentioned?"

Hainsworth asked, pulling a menu closer to him, appearing to study it in his peripheral.

"Oh yes," Art lied as he had never brought it up, not wanting any preferential treatment. "Nice of you to suggest it."

Hainsworth shrugged. "No worries at all."

He looked up at the waitress as she placed a cup of coffee in front of him. "I figured you wanted the usual, Sheriff," she said upon making eye contact.

"Yes, thank you, Barb. And keep it coming." He chuckled. "It was another long night." As the waitress departed, he looked to Art again, adding, "I talked to the judge on the phone yesterday and he said that Mr. Davis has not shown any improvement in the psych ward. I suspect the defence will enter a plea of not guilty by way of insanity. That is of course if he is even fit for trial."

"We won't know that for months," Art replied, taking a sip of his coffee, his face souring due to the heat. "Nothing slower than the wheels of justice."

"Ain't that the truth," Hainsworth said, pouring some milk into his coffee. "But I forwarded your phone number to the court so when it's time to serve as a witness they will give you a ring. But of course, this is all old hat to you."

"I know my way around a courtroom," Art replied, more to himself than to the man across from him. "But that was when I was having to explain my actions as an officer, never as a civilian witness. I suspect it will be easier without the public and the lawyers second guessing your every action."

Hainsworth smirked. "My court experience has been relatively one note. Some drunk drivers here, domestics there."

Art sipped his coffee. "What do they always say, 'As long as you acted in good faith and didn't cause more harm than good, you have nothing to worry about.' Is that it?"

Hainsworth nodded but appeared to look through Art for a

moment. He blinked, readjusting himself in the booth before saying, "I called this little breakfast meeting because I wanted to ask you something."

"What would that be?" Art asked, a coy look appearing on his face.

"I'm starving for good people. My deputies are fine, some better than others. But they are all from here or the next town over. I want someone with real experience, a real eye for the details. A passion for policing."

He held up a hand as Art opened his mouth to interject. "I know you're retired, but this would be a part-time thing only. A couple days a week, or a handful of days a month. We can work out the details later. I just want someone I can bounce stuff off of and that particular someone not be twenty years my junior. To be honest, I'm still mad at myself for brushing you off. You were right about Mr. Davis, and you put everything together yourself. That's the kind of person I need on my team up here."

"I'm flattered, Sheriff. Really, I am. But I promised myself that I would be in my kids' lives more, and I've been doing that ever since I retired. It didn't save my marriage—can't save something that never had a prayer—but my relationship with my boys has grown immensely."

"Exactly, so you move 'em up here, work one day a week, come out for the bigger stuff like the robberies or hunting accidents and enjoy the quiet pace."

Art chuckled. "You don't have kids, do you?"

"No, can't say I do."

"Kids complicate everything. To get primary custody of them would be impossible and even if I did, that would be a big deal to have them change schools and cities and the visitation with their mother so many hours away would be a nightmare."

Hainsworth nodded to himself. "I hear ya, but I just want you to know the option is there."

"I'll tell you what, Sheriff. I go on a fishing trip with my boys next week. I'll think about it while I'm out on the lake. I promise."

Hainsworth raised an eyebrow as if to say, "I already know the answer will be no."

There was a lull in the conversation until Art spoke up. "Any idea what happened to Everette after the hospital? You made it sound like you had a notion on the phone, but you never told me."

Hainsworth's eyes darted around for a moment. He appeared to mull something over in his mind before finally saying, "No. No idea. Some people just can't handle being behind bars." He paused and then added, "But maybe the fact that he killed his mistress finally caught up with him."

Art tilted his head, suspecting that Hainsworth wished to say more, but as Art waited for him to elaborate, the conversation faded again. In the silence Art pondered if he should press the subject. He could see Hainsworth was wrestling with something internally, but the man clearly wished to keep it to himself.

I doubt they've ever come across anything like this as long as he's been sheriff. It's a lot to take, Art thought. *I've seen this enough from other officers that if he wants to talk about it, he will. No good to press him, it will just make him relive the whole thing and...*

He found his mind venturing dangerously close to a painful memory involving a former partner from many years prior.

Art blinked, clearing the sad memories from his mind before saying, "Crappy weather, isn't it?" Art knew the statement was nothing more than small talk, but he wished to slice through the awkward silence.

"I never minded the rain." Hainsworth's face softened as he admired the various raindrops that collected on the windowsill.

He took a sip of coffee, leaned back into the booth and said, "So tell me about that fishing trip with your boys you have planned."

Art moved the tent flap out of the way and blinked at the sunlight that creeped over the surrounding hills. He heard the sound of a loon call out from the distant recesses of the lake and looked to the heart of the still water where his two sons sat fishing in a small rowboat. The orange of their life jackets matched the colour of the leaves that coated the distant bank.

He stretched after having taken an afternoon nap and felt that everything couldn't be better. He looked to his right and saw his truck was still parked off to the side of the trail, his boat trailer still hitched up, ready to make the journey several hours north after the long weekend was over.

Winter would not come here for several weeks.

He moved over to the struggling fire and added a small log, pushing the ashes around with a nearby stick. He admired the end of the twig where white residue remained of the two dozen marshmallows his younger son had roasted in the fire the night prior.

Satisfied that the flame would survive without his attention for several minutes, he grabbed a kettle from the travel bag beside him and hung it over the small fire, pouring a bottle of water into it shortly after.

Art moved about the campsite, tidying up the left-over utensils from breakfast and moving a few beer cans that sat beside a folding chair. He listened to the sounds of the birds chirping overhead and took a moment to appreciate them.

He took several soothing breaths, realizing that he hadn't had a chance to consciously do so in many weeks. With each exhale he attempted to dislodge a small piece of the mental baggage he carried with him.

As the breaths left his lungs, he felt his heartbeat soften. He walked for several minutes, breathing in and out, appreciating the nature around him.

His relaxation was cut short as the beginning sounds of the screeching kettle entered his ears. Art pivoted and moved toward the campsite, realizing he had walked farther than he had realized.

Art removed the kettle from its cradle over the fire and poured it into his camping mug that contained a spoonful of instant coffee. He stirred the mixture around as he listened to the sounds of the flowing water.

He sat down and took in the smell of the coffee, the scent triggering the memory from several weeks earlier, when Sheriff Hainsworth had asked him if he would consider moving to Heartford Meadow.

Art watched as his eldest son reeled the line in and fought with the rod before coming up with an empty hook. Art blew on his coffee as he recalled his response to Sheriff Hainsworth. Seeing his boys out on the water now just reinforced that answer.

He stayed there for a long while until it came time to top off his coffee. He frowned that the kettle was empty and placed his mug beside him, pouring more water into the kettle. Art looked to his sons as his youngest pointed to something in the water and his eldest shifted his position in the boat to admire it as well.

Several seconds passed and Art felt an emotional tug on his heart as he appreciated everything going on. The beauty of the lake; his children being so content, young and full of life.

His eldest son looked toward the shore and waved in Art's direction. His youngest tore his eyes from whatever they were looking at and waved as well. Art waved back and thought about how in a few short years, they would be all grown up, off to high school, jobs and then kids of their own.

He stood up and moved toward the sandy shore. His children cast their lines in the water once more and resumed their fishing expedition.

Art could see in his peripheral that the sand beside him was disturbed in a peculiar way. It looked like someone had written something with their finger. He focused on the letters and read the etched words aloud:

"Thank you for finding me."

Art watched as the water moved over the words with each wave covering the writing, slowly removing it from existence.

As the water rolled over the words one last time, he took a deep breath and felt the life in it. He watched his sons fish until the kettle boiled behind him.

A Note From the Author:

This novella was birthed from a vague idea that I ended up abandoning very early on. While the setting was consistent, the overall plot couldn't have been more different. Originally the character who ended up becoming Everette would have been stalked by a crazed man living in the nearby woods. I lost interest in this premise almost immediately, seeing it for the uninspired notion that it was.

The first few pages where Everette talks to Red on the phone was all there was to the story for several weeks as I focused on writing other things. That is until I found my thoughts returning to the sliver of an idea and my muse pushed forward the concept of introducing a character that wasn't supposed to be there.

The creation of the Art Billings character blew the doors to this project wide open. It was he that drove me around that town, guiding me along those rainswept streets. His idea to ask the sheriff about Everette's criminal history, and most importantly, his intuition that led to him investigating the woods and ultimately finding the body buried within it.

A Note From the Author:

Major portions of this story came to be with no prior guidance from me. I'm reminded of an interview comic and director Jordan Peel gave where he stated his favorite part of the writing process was discovering the answers organically. He too was striving to discover what happened next, just as I did with this story. At multiple points in the writing process, I would complete a handful of pages, feeling very content with what I had written for the day and with no idea what would happen next. Then within an hour or two I would have another scene constructed in my head and the need to get the words down was infectious.

This train of thought brings me to the saga that was constructing the ending. The conclusion went through the most changes from the first draft than anything I have written before. Originally the story concluded with Everette losing his mind in the cell, but I felt that it didn't offer closure to any of the other characters. While it ended the tale with a bang, I felt it left the story lacking.

After typing out the story, I added the scene with Sheriff Hainsworth seeing Gloria in the CCTV recordings. I liked that ending and was proud of it, but I couldn't shake the feeling that the story was leaving Art Billings "out to dry" so to speak, and robbing him of a satisfying conclusion. Through this need, I concocted the fishing trip scene.

The original version of the fishing trip contained more flashbacks to his meeting with Hainsworth, and while I liked the scene, I thought the number of flashbacks made it very clunky to read. I decided a better ending would be to show the flashbacks occurring in real time, so we could see Hainsworth and Art interacting one last time. The last line of the scene, "Tell me about that fishing trip with your boys you have planned," would then have served as a reference to the fishing trip ending as that scene would have then gotten the axe.

But despite this plan, I liked the fishing trip ending and felt it had a lot of life. I decided that I would keep it in some way by reassigning it to this author's note, giving you, the reader, a preview into what Art was up to after the story. Like most plans, that didn't last very long either.

The more I thought about it, the more I believed the fishing trip ending was the true closing passage. People would read it in the author's note and just put it in their head that that's what happened to Art anyways. So, after some hemming and hawing I decided I might as well include the fishing trip ending as part of the main story since it was already the ending in everything but name anyway. I tweaked it a bit to remove the flashbacks and some other inward retrospectives and added the writing in the sand to connect everything together in a neat little package.

While that covers what I wanted to say about the plot beats, there is still the matter of the title. *Nebulous Seas* was never meant to be this novella's name, and was supposed to remain as a working title until I came up with something more fitting. However, the title clung on, and I began to feel that it really helped drive the underlying themes home.

I wanted this story to ground the reader in the setting, a place that you could imagine finding yourself in. I wanted you to feel the chilly autumn air, smell the crisp lake water, and taste the freshly brewed coffee. I'm unsure if I was successful in this regard and maybe it is confirmation bias, but I feel the title captures what I was trying to do more so than something like "The Cabin" or "The Woman on the Porch" ever could.

--Robert J Bradshaw
October 2023

Also by Robert J. Bradshaw

Songs of the Abyss:

A creature that hates to be watched, a forest full of shapeshifting beings, and a war where the ordnance being dropped aren't bombs, but nightmares.

Ten stories of stunning science fiction, otherworldly horrors, and thrilling suspense. All coming together to form a collection like no other.

Get your copy, today!

Shadows At Midnight:

A Mayan ruin with a long-forgotten secret, a cult that is attempting to bridge the gap between worlds, and a beast that lurks inside the phone lines...

In this collection of tales, the mysteries only get darker.

Stories of horrors lurking in the depths, science fiction beyond imagination and pulse pounding thrills, coming together to create an anthology you won't be forgetting anytime soon.

Get your copy, today!

A Monarch Among Kings:

Far off in the Andromeda Galaxy, thousands of colonists have carved out a life for themselves on the remote world of Seryhenya.

However, as a young officer in the Colonial Guard Corps will soon discover, the planet might just hold more life than expected...

Follow multiple viewpoints as each character struggles to navigate the unfolding crisis. Some want to destroy this potential threat before it can fester; others want to live and let live. It is up for debate who is correct in their assessment of the situation.

But keeping an eye on the horizon might not be the only thing the colonists have to worry about...

Get your copy, today!

A Stone's Throw Away From Paradise:

A research vessel is tasked with locating the end of space. A fully-terraformed Mars is not enough to combat the dreaded midlife crisis. An alien race believes it is their civilization's mission to uplift any life it encounters.

Bradshaw's latest anthology contains twelve stories of thrilling science fiction that will bring you to the distant future, the long-forgotten past, and everywhere in between.

In this collection of short stories, technological expansion, ghosts in the machine, and the meaning of the soul are only the beginning...

Get your copy, today!

About the Author

Robert J. Bradshaw was born and raised in St. Catharines, Ontario, Canada. He relocated to British Columbia, seeking adventure. He currently lives in the Fraser Valley region.

Nebulous Seas is Bradshaw's fifth release to date. His other works include the anthologies *Songs of the Abyss* (released in 2020), *Shadows At Midnight* (released in 2021) and *A Stone's Throw Away From Paradise* (released in 2023). His debut novel, *A Monarch Among Kings,* a science fiction colonization epic, was released in 2022.

Bradshaw is currently hard at work on his sophomore novel, as well as another gathering of tales.

Printed in Great Britain
by Amazon